Rachel and Her Mother

Or, the Public Trial of Martin Heidegger

a play in two acts

Rachel and Her Mother

Or, the Public Trial of Martin Heidegger

a play in two acts

Caroll Thomas Jacobs

First Printing: April 2020

ISBN 978-0-9991187-9-5 paperback

Available as a paperback and ebook, online

Cover image credit: Photo of Hannah Arendt at age eight with her mother, 1914. Public domain. From Wikimedia.

CAST

Rachel, A woman, nineteen years old. A student in post-World-War I Germany.

Hannah Arendt, A woman, eighteen, who is also a student.

Martin Heidegger, A male philosopher, thirty-five years old. He is a short, powerful, and charismatic professor at Marburg University in 1924.

Rachel's Father, Professor Gershon at Yeshiva University.

Steven Baker, Rachel's beau, a science professor at Yeshiva University.

Karl Jaspers, A large, friendly man in his 40's. A philosopher.

Rachel's Mother, In ghost form.

ACT II 115

ACT I

Scene 1 Rachel's apartment

(Rachel is in her apartment, in semi-darkness. She sits at a desk illuminated by a lamp. Holding a telephone, she waits. At last, she begins to speak, but not into the phone.)

RACHEL

It's me again, Mama. I need to talk to you. I've begun work on my dissertation.

(pause)

I have so many questions about my life. Am I going too far, too fast? I'd like to open a new door, but maybe I should just try to close the old one, the one which allowed the evil into our lives and changed your life, and mine, forever. I'm having bad dreams. Am I on the way to losing myself?

(pause)

The trouble is, Mama, I think I'm beginning to understand. But must your Ruchele be dragged out of her head to be free?

(pause)

Papa can't admit I have a mind of my own. I do, and I intend to use it. For you. For us, Mama. He hates Martin Heidegger, and he cannot bring himself to like Hannah. She's my intellectual partner. As for Heidegger? He's still standing. Holding the old door open. Evil is not through with us. The truth is, Mama, I'm no match for the most metaphysical of men.

(Rachel returns phone to its base; lights up)

Scene 2 Lecture hall

(Heidegger strides down-stage center and addresses the audience as his students. It is 1924, a cold, rainy morning in November. This is Rachel's Ph.D. research. We will move back and forth in time. In the front row are Rachel and the young Hannah They listen and take notes.

HEIDEGGER

There are a few hooks on the back wall to hang your wet coats. It's cold and damp inside, too. There will be no heat again, and no lights. The Rector of Marburg University sends his apologies. You may have difficulty taking notes. If so, listen. And try to remember.

(pause)

There WERE better days in Germany, once upon a time. Six

hard years have passed since The Great War ended. We live with promises. Waiting, in near darkness, in this classroom, I only promise that we will do philosophy. The apostle Paul said philosophy is foolishness. And so it is, unless we ask the most important question a philosopher can ask: What is Being? Neither scientists nor theologians, and certainly not politicians, can answer that question. Being can only be grasped by THINKING it. So, let us begin our understanding here, in this room.

(pause)

Being is absent from our lives. Why? For twenty-five hundred years we have forgotten it. We EXIST, yes, but without the passion and purpose which only a connection with Being can bring. A religious leader might say to us: you have forgotten God, and that is why you despair, that is why you have too little food, not enough energy for heat and lights, not enough funds for you to attend the University. Oh, yes, we Germans suffer because we are also victims of Versailles. Reparations. The endless outflow of life-giving resources to French and especially English blood-suckers. A religious leader would remind us that we must have sinned. You might believe it if you believe the Fairytale that is Christian doctrine. Our failure is not sin. Our failure is that we have forgotten Being. We have slumped into an Everydayness that aims no higher than to be Average. That goal satisfies our social liberals and those who want to reduce Germany to a spineless democracy. In truth, we sleep, unaware of our True Identity, of who we should and must Be. In these lectures, I will try to awaken you. Is it important to wake from our forgetfulness of Being? You decide. Without Being we Germans are not A People, and Germany is not A Nation. Without Being, whose very essence is Time Itself, YOU have no continuity as a person, WE have no continuity as a people and GERMANY is without a destiny. Nietzsche came to offer us the glad tidings: God is dead. What does that mean? Quite simply, it means that our Judeo-Christian Culture has come to an end. I will try to return us to a future which we can grasp as our new beginning.

(he pauses to survey the students)

Many of you are shivering to warm yourselves. You can't think under these circumstances. I apologize. I'll end the lecture here.

(he closes his lecture book)

You know my office hours. If you have questions, come and see me.

(Hannah and Rachel rise. Hannah steps forward to talk to Heidegger as he turns to walk away)

HANNAH

(Shy, but determined)

Professor! Professor Heidegger!

(He turns to listen)

May I come to your office tomorrow?

HEIDEGGER

(Opening his lecture book)

You are Fraulein...

HANNAH

Arendt. Hannah Arendt.

HEIDEGGER

(Jotting down her name and the time)

Yes, yes. The infamous Fraulein Arendt.

(Looks at her closely)

Lovely ribbons to tie her hair back. You may come at 3:30.
Thursday.

(Crosses to his office area.)

RACHEL

(To Hannah)

What presence! His words seem to flow from a deep well of
fresh insights

HANNAH

We call him "The Little Magician from Messkirch." He is so
serious, so persuasive. We feel that he knows the secret of
Human Existence.

RACHEL

You and Germany need the hope he brings.

(Hannah nods)

Which of his thoughts inspire you most?

HANNAH

Each of us, he says, constructs who we are by our choosing
to Be.

RACHEL

That's a directive for young people to take charge of their
lives, isn't it?

HANNAH

His students feel it as a moral command.

RACHEL

Was he clear HOW you should achieve Being?

HANNAH
No, but he is opening the door for each of us to understand.
He will guide us through dark times.

Scene 3 Heidegger's office

(Hannah crosses toward Heidegger's office, pauses to untie the ribbon holding her hair back, and shakes her hair out.

Rachel sits at her desk. Steven enters. She brings up the music on a CD; they have a few sexy, wordless moments dancing without talking or touching. Heidegger opens door to Hannah. Rachel turns to watch them.)

HEIDEGGER

Come in, please.

(Hannah timidly walks into the office area and stands, hesitating)

Where are you from, Fraulein?

HANNAH

Koenigsberg.

HEIDEGGER

That makes you special. Koenigsberg! City of Emanuel Kant. Is that how you come to have an interest in philosophy?

HANNAH
I came to Marburg because of you.

HEIDEGGER

What a flatterer you are, Fraulein Arendt! Before we discuss what is on your mind, please tell me a little about yourself.

> (Lights dim in their area; no talking is heard, but they are seen talking; he gestures, she stands shyly.

Scene 4 Rachel's room

> (Rachel is sitting at her desk, working. She doesn't notice her father coming toward her. She is startled to see him)

RACHEL

Are you spying on me?

FATHER

Spying? Rachel, I'm your father! Your health and welfare are of the first importance to me. How are you getting on with your work?

RACHEL

It's going well.

FATHER

I don't see much of you these days. Maybe you'd like to come home for dinner. Tomorrow. It's the Sabbath.

RACHEL

I can't.

FATHER

It would make me happy, Rachel.

RACHEL

I don't mean to make you unhappy, Papa. I have work to do. You're interrupting me now.

(Raises her notebook, points to Hannah and Heidegger.)

FATHER

It's the Sabbath.

RACHEL

God will understand.

FATHER

Nothing is more important than observing the Sabbath.

RACHEL

Papa. You promised not to interfere!

FATHER

I'm only doing what is commanded of me.

RACHEL

I understand. Your work is God's work. But, please allow me to handle my family responsibilities in my own way.

FATHER

Yes. Of course. You're right about that.

(pauses)

I have a letter from your uncle Max in Jerusalem. He has a proposal for you.

RACHEL

He's found someone to marry me!

FATHER

No. No, Rachel. There's a fantastic career opportunity at the University of Jerusalem. They're looking for an assistant director of Education. After a year or two, you could be the head of the department.

RACHEL

I can't complete my studies there.

FATHER

You don't need a Ph.D. in philosophy to plan the education of young people from all over the world for a life in Israel.

RACHEL

That could be very exciting.

FATHER

It's a job made for you. We have to let your uncle Max know as soon as possible.

RACHEL

Papa, don't rush me. I've already begun my dissertation.

FATHER

Think about it, Ruchele! One day you will be a great professor of Jewish Culture and Thought!

RACHEL

(Holds up her hand)

Wait! Stop right there. Who I will be is my concern. And, I'm Rachel, not Little Ruchele!

FATHER

Listen. Listen to me carefully. I want you to be you. But, without ties to your religion, your family, your people, your culture, who are you?

RACHEL

(Sighs deeply, lowers her head, and is silent,
weary from arguing)

That question torments me, Papa.

FATHER

Your identity was fixed before you were born. We and God
saw to that.

RACHEL

Since my identity and my destiny are on a stone tablet some
place, you needn't have fears about what I'm thinking.

FATHER

God and I know who you are. You're a Jew. It is YOUR job
not to forget.

RACHEL

When did God decide I was to be a Jew?

FATHER

Don't get philosophical with me! You know what I mean.
Don't pursue Martin Heidegger, a German, a man obsessed
with all that philosophical craziness about BEING! And
Hannah Arendt? She was more GERMAN than Jew!

RACHEL

She chose to think! And act! That made her different!

FATHER

She betrayed her people!

RACHEL

That's YOUR opinion!

FATHER

Everybody knows, Rachel! The dirt is out on Hannah and Martin Heidegger.

RACHEL

Hannah is a major political thinker. I want to know the truth about Martin Heidegger, including his revelation of Being. And I'm not alone in believing he is the most important philosopher of the 20th century.

FATHER

Hannah Arendt was a stateless Jew! But you're right about Martin Heidegger. He is the most important philosopher of the 20th century... to join the Nazi Party!

RACHEL

Papa, my aim is to get to the bottom of what he did.

FATHER

He gave up his faith in God.

RACHEL

So did Mama!

FATHER

She didn't know what she was doing! Her family was destroyed. She never recovered.
I tell you she didn't know what she was saying.

RACHEL

She did, Papa. She did. I had long, long talks with her. At night, when you were asleep.

(Begins to cry)

FATHER

Rachel, your Mother is dead.

(Goes to her, holds her close)

I miss her too, Ruchele. I'm asking you again. Please let her go.

RACHEL

I can't, Papa. She's inside me. Here...

(Holds her hands to the sides of her head)

I hear her crying. I feel her suffering, still.

FATHER

Let her go, Ruchele.

> (Long pause. Releases her and turns to leave,
> then wheels around)

Rachel, are you seeing someone?

> (She looks at him uncomprehending)

Is it someone at the University?

> (She remains silent, staring at him)

I'm not the only one there who has eyes!

RACHEL

Now I understand what you're doing! You pulled your
Israeli strings. Uncle Max got me the offer in Jerusalem!

FATHER

I'm trying to be helpful!

RACHEL

Controlling my life is not helpful!

> (Crosses to the office area where Hannah and
> Heidegger continue talking. Her father
> leaves.)

Scene 5 Heidegger's Office

HEIDEGGER

You are unusually well-prepared in philosophy for such a young woman.

HANNAH

I read philosophy on my own, and I also audited courses in philosophy and theology when we moved to Berlin.

HEIDEGGER

Then you came to Marburg. Because of me.

HANNAH
There is talk you'll become world-famous one day.

HEIDEGGER
Who talks that way about me?

HANNAH
My Koenigsberger friend, Heinrich. He's here at the University.

HEIDEGGER

And he's predicting great things of me?

HANNAH

Professor Bultmann and other professors say it too.

HEIDEGGER

It's kind of you, all of you, to think of me in that way. Thank you. Now tell me, how can I help you?

HANNAH

I don't understand what you are saying about Being.

HEIDEGGER

Did you read Parmenides, as I asked?

HANNAH

I did. It seems to me you agree with Parmenides that Being and Thought are closely connected.

HEIDEGGER

You'll learn how closely Being, thought, and language are related as we proceed. Being cannot be far off if we THINK it. Think about that.

HANNAH
What about the rest of Parmenides?

HEIDEGGER

You may forget it.

HANNAH

What about the rest of your lecture? Should I forget it?

HEIDEGGER

(Pauses and eyes her briefly, noting her provocative remark.)

You and Being are mysteriously connected when you THINK philosophically. There are only two languages in which such thinking can occur and you are expert in both: Greek and German.

HANNAH

The poor French! I wonder why they bother.

HEIDEGGER

(Taken aback)

Fraulein Arendt, the English and the Americans also bother, as you say, with philosophy. Have you evidence that they, or the French, are successful in illuminating Being?

HANNAH

I apologize, Professor Heidegger. My remark about the French was intended to provoke a smile. I'm a little nervous. I so wanted to make a good impression.

HEIDEGGER

You have. You have, indeed. Don't be nervous. Tell me. What stands out in my lecture, so far?

HANNAH

You talk about Being, but the connections between Being and Thought, or Being and Time, elude me.

HEIDEGGER

You're certain about that?

HANNAH

I know when I don't know something.

HEIDEGGER

You're cautious, careful, and frank. You may become a great philosopher yourself, Fraulein Arendt. Professor Bultmann tells me you're interested in Theology, that you are rather outspoken in your ways, and that you know Latin, but especially Greek, very well. Is that correct?

HANNAH

Professor Bultmann spoke to you about me? He told you I was outspoken?

HEIDEGGER

Your fame runs before you. He said on the first day you made it clear that you wouldn't tolerate any anti-Semitic remarks in class.

(She nods cautiously)

May I ask if he's behaving himself?

HANNAH

He hasn't offended in any way.

HEIDEGGER

Did I offend you by my remarks about religion?

HANNAH

No. I'm not religious.

HEIDEGGER

Well, then, you have a mind that is OPEN. In fact, you have a spirited and curious mind.

HANNAH

You're very kind.

HEIDEGGER

I see you as a very special person, Fraulein Arendt. I'd like to give you special attention. With your consent.

HANNAH

Special attention?

(She reflects on the romantic innuendo.)

That would be wonderful! Of course, you have my consent!

HEIDEGGER

It's settled, then. Now, tell me about your living arrangements. Where do you live?

HANNAH

Marburger Strasse. I have an attic room.

HEIDEGGER

Do you have heat?

HANNAH

The heat rises up the stairwell from the lower floors and it's almost comfortable.

HEIDEGGER

Can you cook there?

HANNAH

If I wish to. My light must be out by 11 PM. I use candles to read by.

HEIDEGGER

Sounds luxurious! Do you have company? I mean, do other students come to study and talk philosophy with you at night?

HANNAH

Frau Moeller does not allow students to visit in the evening hours. After 6 PM. No parties are allowed. But I have company.

HEIDEGGER

You break the rules?

HANNAH

I have a secret visitor after hours.

HEIDEGGER

(Looks startled)

A lover?

HANNAH

A mouse!

HEIDEGGER

Oh, a pet!

HANNAH

No, not a pet. My little mouse visits late at night. He comes out of a hole across from my bed. When I see him in the opening, I'm ready with something for him to eat. Gently, ever so gently, I coax him to come out so we can talk philosophy.

HEIDEGGER

You talk philosophy with a mouse? I don't believe you!

HANNAH

If you don't believe me, come and see for yourself!

(Correcting herself)

I didn't mean...

HEIDEGGER

I'm hoping you DO mean to invite me to visit you and your philosophic friend. Do you think I should, after hours?

HANNAH

(Pauses.)

If you wish to.

HEIDEGGER

You are sure?

HANNAH

You MUST if you want to see my philosophic friend!

HEIDEGGER

Tomorrow evening at ten?

HANNAH

I'll expect you.

>(Lights dim; Hannah crosses to
>Rachel's room. Rachel is waiting.
>Heidegger primps for his meeting
>with Hannah)

Scene 6 Rachel's Room

RACHEL

How exciting!

HANNAH

I could hardly breathe in his presence.

RACHEL

That's how it began?

HANNAH

Yes.

RACHEL

He showed more than a little interest in you! You invited him to your attic?

HANNAH

He was dying to come.

RACHEL

I knew it.

(Confiding)

I have a secret, too. I've been seeing someone for quite some time.

HANNAH

Tell me.

RACHEL

He's handsome. Intelligent. A professor of science at Yeshiva University. He seems to be free of the philosophical problems that tie my emotions in knots. We have dinner in his apartment. I can't stop thinking about him.

(Hannah begins to primp; she nervously checks her watch)

Hannah, it means a great deal to me to learn that you broke the rules; that you met Martin Heidegger alone in your attic.

Scene 7 Hannah's room

(Heidegger knocks on the attic door)

HANNAH

I was afraid you weren't coming. It's almost eleven.

HEIDEGGER

I apologize for being late.

>   (Hannah waits for an explanation which
>   doesn't come, then smiles)

HANNAH

Welcome to my luxurious suite! Monsieur, there's my bed! Over there is my chair for special guests, such as yourself! My night table, my book case, and the little hole, right over there, is where my night visitor lives and thinks, philosophically, about my existence!

HEIDEGGER

It's even grander than I expected! I brought you this.

>   (Hands her a book; she's surprised and
>   shows delight)

HANNAH

Holderlin!

HEIDEGGER

I hope you don't have a copy.

HANNAH

No, I don't!

HEIDEGGER

May I?
                    (Takes the book, opens it.)

This is from his poem "Bread and Wine."

> We have come too late. Though the gods are living
> Over our heads, up in a different world
> Endlessly there they act and
> Little they seem to care whether we live or do not
> Night and distress make us strong.

HANNAH

The words, or perhaps it is your way in delivering them,
convey strong feelings of alienation, abandonment,
hopelessness.

HEIDEGGER

A disconnection with Being. At this particular time in our
history, one can only feel despair and wait.

HANNAH

What are we waiting for?

HEIDEGGER

The return of the gods. The gods serve as metaphors for Being in Holderlin's poetry.

HANNAH

Do you ever give your mind a rest from thinking such serious thoughts?

HEIDEGGER

Entangled in the world of the here and now… Alive, without Being, in the face of death and Nothingness is terrifying.

HANNAH

I protest! May I protest? Alive in a world shared with others can be wonderful! Joyful, too.

HEIDEGGER

I'm sure it can.

HANNAH

Don't you ever seek the lighter side of life?

HEIDEGGER

Of course not. Do I look unhappy?

HANNAH

No. You look preoccupied.

(Pauses)

We're rule-breakers, aren't we!

HEIDEGGER

Philosophers live on a different plane from ordinary people.

HANNAH

(She removes the scarf from around his neck; takes his arm and leads him to the chair near the bed; she sits on bed)

Tell me a little about yourself.

HEIDEGGER

You are making fun of our meeting in my office!

(She laughs)

HANNAH

Tell me anyway.

HEIDEGGER

I'm from generations of hard-working farming people. Church-going Catholics. I was on the path to becoming a priest, but turned from The Faith to philosophy. Now, I'm devoted to philosophy, alone.

HANNAH

Devoted to Being and philosophy as passionately as you were to God and theology?

HEIDEGGER

Even more.

HANNAH

You have assured yourself a life of great seriousness.

HEIDEGGER

(Picks up a book from the bedside table)

Rilke is your favorite poet?

HANNAH

One of my favorites.

HEIDEGGER

Read something you like.

(Hands her the book)

HANNAH

(Opens it, but looks directly at him)

30

Who, if I cried out, would hear me
among the angels? If one pressed me
to his heart I'd be consumed
in his stronger existence.

Every angel is terrifying.

Whom can I turn to
in my need?

HEIDEGGER

(Takes her hand, looks directly into her eyes)

Are you aware that Rilke used angels as metaphors for
Being?

HANNAH

No. But I feel each moment with you is the beginning of a
new beginning.

HEIDEGGER

Was that the first elegy?

HANNAH

Yes, but somewhat changed.

HEIDEGGER

I know.

HANNAH

I did some editing.

HEIDEGGER

You changed Rilke's poem.

HANNAH

Yes. Now it speaks from MY feelings and to MY imagination.

HEIDEGGER

Hannah, you're remarkable! Do you write poetry or just edit the work of others to suit yourself?

HANNAH

I've written some, too.

HEIDEGGER

May I see it?

HANNAH

If you show me some of yours! You must be guilty of writing poetry!

HEIDEGGER

I'm guilty. Why do we do it?

HANNAH

Sometimes we're sad. In those moments, we just want to talk things over with ourselves.

HEIDEGGER

Or search for words as signs of something unseen.

HANNAH

Your poems are about Being?

HEIDEGGER

And its Truth.

HANNAH

(A bell sounds)

Forgive me, but it's time to light the candles.

> (Lights one candle and Heidegger offers to light another. She gives him the matches, waits, and then turns off the electric light.)

There. It's almost as bright.

HEIDEGGER

And certainly more romantic.

HANNAH

My other guest may appear, now that the light is dimmer.

(Points to a small hole)

Be quite still.

(They silently watch and wait, but the mouse
doesn't come out.)

HEIDEGGER

Have you given your little guest a name?

HANNAH

Yes. I thought of it while waiting for you.

HEIDEGGER

What is it?

HANNAH

BEING.

HEIDEGGER

Wonderful!

(Stands, clapping his hands like a child.)

HANNAH

(Looks directly into his eyes)

I've been waiting for a more personal connection with Being.

HEIDEGGER

Hannah, you're an exotic delight!

> (Crosses to his office and begins
> writing a letter. Hannah and Rachel
> move to center-stage)

Scene 8 Center stage

RACHEL

How did you learn that Professor Heidegger was married and the father of two children?

HANNAH

It isn't a secret. It's of little concern to me.

RACHEL

He visits you in the attic?

HANNAH

We have to be careful. He has a mountain cabin. We'll go there, and he'll tell me about the great work he's writing.

RACHEL

You are his secret inspiration.

HANNAH

He said as much.

(Walks a few steps and turns around.)

How was dinner with your scientist?

RACHEL

He can cook, too!

(Crosses to her room. Rachel's father approaches)

Scene 9 Rachel's room

FATHER

You decided to be with someone rather than with your family during Passover.

(Holds up his hand)

You have the right. Who is he, Rachel?

RACHEL

Professor Baker. He teaches biology and evolutionary theory at Yeshiva University.

FATHER

Is he Jewish?

RACHEL

No.

FATHER

How well do you know him?

RACHEL

Well enough to have dinner with him.

FATHER

Nothing serious?

RACHEL

No, Papa, nothing serious, but I've decided to marry him tomorrow and start having his children.

FATHER

Rachel, don't kill me with your humor!

RACHEL

Papa, why must you see any interest I have in another person as a matter of life and death?

FATHER

Just tell me your interest in this man goes no farther than dinner, occasionally, as a friend.

RACHEL

(Furious)

I will not allow you to talk to me this way! I demand the freedom....

FATHER

You are not free to disobey God!

RACHEL

I thought we ARE free. Free to disobey God and our parents!

FATHER

It is Philosophy that is making your life difficult!

> (Father exits. Hannah, still holding the letter, crosses to Rachel.)

Scene 10 Rachel's room

HANNAH

You look unhappy.

RACHEL

I have family problems. Did your mother know how you
felt about Martin Heidegger in those early days of intimacy?

HANNAH

No.

RACHEL

Would she have cared that he wasn't a Jew?

HANNAH

No. I was free to be with anyone I wished.

RACHEL

And free to marry anyone you chose?

HANNAH

I married twice.

RACHEL

The first time to assert your independence from the Master
from Messkirch?

HANNAH

You could say that. But the second time provided me with the stability which made my everyday life livable.

RACHEL

I understand. Thanks.

> (Hannah crosses to attic, looks at the letter and reads, but it is Heidegger's voice we hear.)

Scene 11 Hannah's room

HEIDEGGER

Meet me on "our bench" at 3 o'clock. I've written a short poem about your eyes. I see you've done something to your hair. It becomes you. Do you think of me at all when we're apart?

> (Unfolds a letter from Hannah who speaks as he pretends to read it)

HANNAH

Thinking of you is all I do. Can't we go to your cabin? The time is right.

HEIDEGGER

This Saturday, take the morning train to Freiburg, then the

afternoon autobus to Todtnauberg. I will be there, waiting for you.

>(Wearing backpacks, Hannah and Heidegger cross to meet; they briefly hold hands and talk as they move in the direction of his cabin)

HANNAH

Were you waiting long?

HEIDEGGER

A painful hour.

HANNAH

Will it take us long to get there?

HEIDEGGER

It will seem like an eternity.

HANNAH

Not if you hold my hand.

HEIDEGGER

We're almost there.

>(Hannah runs ahead and waits; Heidegger opens the door; they enter)

Welcome to my Black Forest Castle!

(She surveys the spare furnishings)

May I point out: the table on which your Professor writes, four chairs, pillows by the fireplace, which are for you, my very special guest, and over there, my lonely bed. I brought candles to light your lovely face.

HANNAH

(Surveying the room)

It's grander than I could ever imagine!

HEIDEGGER

Your coming here, Hannah, fulfills my greatest wish. I kiss your hand.

(She holds out her hand.)

Put your backpack in the corner, make yourself comfortable, and I'll make a fire.

HANNAH

(Holding him back)

You never stop working! Forget the fire! We must celebrate our arrival. Have you a Riesling my Good Professor?

(He pretends to show her the label of the

bottle.)

HANNAH

My favorite!

HEIDEGGER

May I, Mademoiselle?

(Pretends to pour the wine in her glass, and in his.)

To you, my dark-eyed fraulein from Koenigsberg.

HANNAH

To you, Professor Extraordinaire! And to philosophy.

HEIDEGGER

To you, and love. There, I've said it!

HANNAH

Martin? Yes, now I'll call you Martin. And you'll call me Hannah. It's wonderful here. We climbed so high, from the valley, I feel we're on top of your very own mountain!

HEIDEGGER

It's a sacred place up here. Here's where the gods are, and your angels, too. Here poetry and philosophy are coupled and sacred words are born.

HANNAH

Will the words come to us?

HEIDEGGER

Yes, if we are prepared to utter them. Being, using our
language, speaks US.

HANNAH

Please! Don't assail me with words I can't understand!

HEIDEGGER

Your presence warms my soul and gives my heart speech.
Until now, only solitude and thoughts of nature brought
forth words, words I thought true of the Being which I know
and feel.

HANNAH

You won't be alone.

HEIDEGGER

Close your eyes. Think of the universe. Now extend your
thinking to that which surrounds and penetrates it.

HANNAH

(Closes her eyes)

It's difficult, Martin. I'm afraid I'll be lost in Space.

HEIDEGGER

I'll be near you.

HANNAH

(Eyes still closed)

Martin, tell me what you see.

HEIDEGGER

The early morning light quietly growing above the mountains. And you?

HANNAH

(Her eyes still closed; reaches out)

I'm searching for you.

HEIDEGGER

Listen. The little wind-wheel outside the cabin is singing in the gathering thunderstorm.

HANNAH

It'll frighten away the terrors of coming Night.

HEIDEGGER

In early summer, Hannah, the lonely narcissus blooms

hidden in the meadow; the rock-rose gleams under the maple.

HANNAH

(Looks off stage in the direction of the bed)

Look for me in the meadow.

HEIDEGGER

(As she moves away)

The mountain brook in night's stillness is plunging over the boulders.

(He overtakes her)

Should we leave the candles burning?

HANNAH

No. The stars are light enough.

(Begins unbuttoning her blouse)

It's cold.
                    (Puts his arms around her)

HEIDEGGER
You're shaking.

HANNAH

Not from the cold.

> (They move away; lights up on Rachel and her father who has been reading her notes)

Scene 12 Rachel's room

FATHER

How could a Jewish girl do such a thing!

RACHEL

She fell in love with a professor. It can happen.

FATHER

He seduced her!

RACHEL

Love has its ways. Perhaps she seduced him.

FATHER

A man's lust wears many disguises!

RACHEL

Hannah knew what she was doing.

FATHER

She was too young to know. She had no father! She was away from home, away from her mother and family. She was lonely, unprotected, vulnerable. She lost her way.

RACHEL

She got the love she wanted.

FATHER

To her ever-lasting shame.

(Exits; Steven enters)

Scene 13 Rachel's room

STEVEN

When are you going to introduce me to your Mom and Dad?

RACHEL

Mom and Dad? That sounds Middle America.

STEVEN

Now you know.

RACHEL

We're getting along so well. I don't want to spoil it. I don't want it to end.

STEVEN

Then think about marrying me.

RACHEL

Steven, please. I can't handle another major problem in my life right now.

STEVEN

I'm a major problem?

RACHEL

I mean my work. My family.

STEVEN

Your work is coming along fine. Your family might like me! I'm a professor, I make a decent living, I love their daughter. What more could they ask?

RACHEL

My Father's the problem, Steven. My Mother? She's not with us anymore.

(Pause)

Steven, my Mother's dead. I never mentioned it because, first of all, I have pretty deep feelings about her life...and her death. I never intended to get this far in our relationship. I hope you understand.

STEVEN

I don't, of course, but I suppose you will tell me more, later. When you're ready. Your Father was once a practicing Rabbi. He may find me something of a problem.

RACHEL

Teaching at Yeshiva University is very much in your favor, Steven.

STEVEN

So, you'll bring me out of your closet?

RACHEL

I'll seriously think about arranging it. But you mustn't breathe a word about wanting to marry me in Papa's presence. Promise me you'll present yourself as, as a friend, interested in my doctoral work.

STEVEN

I hate deception, Rachel.

RACHEL

Promise me.

STEVEN

Alright. Friend.

> (Steven exits. Rachel turns to study.
> Heidegger and Hannah who are on
> opposite sides of the stage reading
> brief letters and notes to one another)

Scene 14 Opposite sides of stage

HANNAH

Three days have passed and you haven't answered my note.
You didn't look at me in class today. Off you marched. Not a
word. Not even a glance.

HEIDEGGER

You mustn't send me notes without my asking for them.
The risk is too great.

HANNAH

I'm lonely without you. Have you changed your mind? Are
your feelings still the same?

HEIDEGGER

My feelings are unchanged. Please understand that my
mind is occupied with galley proofs.

HANNAH

My mind is occupied with proofs of ever-lasting love. I can't wait to whisper in your ear how I feel about your midnight visit. When can we spend a full weekend in the cabin? I am, forever yours, Hannah.

HEIDEGGER

Hannah, Hannah. You are the passion of my life.

HANNAH

Eight wordless days have passed. Life in me ebbs. I can't eat. Night weighs most heavily on me. I can't breathe. I languish.

HEIDEGGER

Elfrida is beginning to ask questions. We can't meet for a while. Give me three months to mend things and rise above suspicion.

HANNAH

(Screams)

I can't endure THREE months! I want to come out of the Shadows! I can't SHARE you with Elfrida. I can't live without you. Who when I cry will hear me among the angels?

HEIDEGGER

Wait. Wait. Wait. I have too much to lose if we're exposed. I can't come under suspicion now. My book will be published shortly, and I'll be offered the chair in philosophy at Freiburg. Husserl told me so!

HANNAH

Can't we go to Freiburg together?

HEIDEGGER

Hannah, my Hannah. Come to your senses! A scandal in my domestic life would end my career!

(Rachel, seeing Hannah distraught, goes to her)

RACHEL

Can I be of help?

HANNAH

Become an angel. Change my life, as gods and angels can.

RACHEL

You know I can't.

HANNAH

It's helpful that you understand how I feel.

RACHEL

What will you do?

HANNAH

I can't say no to a self that hopes. That is the way I am.

RACHEL

Does Martin care?

HANNAH

Yes.

RACHEL

What will he do?

HANNAH

He wants me to meet him on our bench near the University at 7 this evening.

(Hannah and Heidegger cross to center)

Scene 15 Center stage

HEIDEGGER

I have good news.

(Hannah's face brightens.)

HANNAH

You're leaving Elfrida!

HEIDEGGER

Have you lost your mind?

HANNAH

Forgive me for hoping.

HEIDEGGER

It's confirmed. I will be the new chairman of the department of philosophy at the University of Freiburg!

HANNAH

Should I congratulate you?

HEIDEGGER

You don't have to be happy for me, Hannah.

HANNAH

If I were not so unhappy BECAUSE of you, Martin, I would be happy for you.

HEIDEGGER

You resent my success!

HANNAH

I am saddened by your neglect and insensitivity!

HEIDEGGER

You're angry.

HANNAH

(She clinches her fists and shouts)

YES! I'M ANGRY! You have a responsibility to the decision we made to love one another! You have a responsibility to your own feelings, and to mine as well!

HEIDEGGER

Why are you speaking to me this way? I only ask you to understand, but apparently you can't!

HANNAH

Understanding only makes it worse.

HEIDEGGER

I'm asking you, now, to be patient. Until I get settled in Freiburg. Then we can continue.

HANNAH

I can continue being your, your STUDENT there!

HEIDEGGER

Hannah, even that is too risky. I've made a decision. You must do your doctoral work with someone else. I'll write Karl Jaspers. He'll take you on if I ask him.

HANNAH

(Stunned)

You want me to leave.

HEIDEGGER

I'll write you when we can meet.

HANNAH

Martin? Do you love me?

HEIDEGGER

I've told you, you're the passion of my life.

HANNAH

Then find a way for us to be together.

HEIDEGGER

You must be patient!

HANNAH

I will be patient. Just tell me my patience will be rewarded.

HEIDEGGER

I can tell you; you'll remain my secret passion, forever.

HANNAH

What a lovely thought, Martin. Such devotion to the romantic. The best in life will remain hidden, a secret to be enjoyed, at night. Isn't such a life rather like that of my little mouse? He goes, then comes in the evening hours because he wants what I have to offer.

HEIDEGGER

I must catch a train at 8 o'clock.

HANNAH

(Looks at her watch, walks a few steps, stops, then suddenly CRIES OUT as if mortally wounded:)

I hate you with all my heart!

HEIDEGGER

(Gently)

I'll take you home.

HANNAH

Will you stay with me?

HEIDEGGER

Yes, for as long as I can.

> (Lights up on Rachel and Steven in
> her apartment. Music is playing.
> They're somewhat disheveled.
> Rachel's Father unexpectedly enters)

Scene 16 Rachel's apartment

FATHER

Rachel...?

RACHEL

Papa! Papa, this is Doctor Steven Baker.

STEVEN

> (Steven holds out his hand. Her Father moves
> toward him)

I'm very pleased to meet you Doctor Gershon.

> (Extends his hand)

Rachel has told me a lot about you and the courses you
teach.

FATHER

(Doesn't shake Steven's hand)

You're new to our faculty.

STEVEN

Yes, I am.

FATHER

Rachel tells me you're interested in evolutionary theory.

STEVEN

That's right.

FATHER

She also tells me you're interested in her doctoral work.

(Rachel, nervous, moves closer to Steven)

RACHEL

Steven knows science and a lot about philosophy, too.

STEVEN

You have a bright and wonderful daughter, Doctor Gershon. You must be very proud. I would be crazy not to be interested in helping her in any way I can.

FATHER

Professor Baker, may I ask, are you happy at Yeshiva University?

STEVEN

I am. Why do you ask?

FATHER

Well, the education you provide is secondary to the religious and cultural education which conveys our root values.

STEVEN

I have a deep respect for Jewish religious and cultural traditions.

FATHER

Did you study those traditions in college?

STEVEN

No. Although I'm not, as you say, conveying your root values, I have something important to teach Yeshiva students.

FATHER

Darwin is not of the first importance.

STEVEN

I'm not aiming to produce evolutionary theorists.

FATHER

Still, you want to influence our students in the direction of your science.

STEVEN

Of course.

FATHER

Are you religious?

STEVEN

No.

FATHER

Where is your identity as a person?

STEVEN

I'm a mixed bag of genes as we all are. I'm just plain American.

FATHER

Is that an identity?

STEVEN

Perhaps not.

FATHER

Rachel has an identity. She's a link in a long chain of people who have a distinct history. That history is a moving reality, cemented by a covenant with God. Without undue influences, Rachel and her children will continue in that long chain and extend that history.

STEVEN

I'm aware of who Rachel is.

FATHER

Good. I trust you are not thinking of Rachel in some more intimate way.

STEVEN

I would like to!

(Turns to look at Rachel who cannot believe his response)

FATHER

No, Dr. Baker. You must not think in those terms.

STEVEN

Rachel is an adult.
(Rachel walks away)

FATHER

You must not think of Rachel in those terms.

(Steven looks forlorn)

Are you feeling excluded?

STEVEN

Yes.

FATHER

I mean no offense. Forgive me for saying it, but you ARE excluded.

STEVEN

Are you telling me to stay away from Rachel?

FATHER

Not at all, Dr. Baker. Rachel likes, and respects, you. You have every reason to be around her, to appreciate her for Who She Is. Be friends. That's what I am saying.

RACHEL

(She can take no more of this)

Papa, Steven and I have to leave.

(She takes his hand)

FATHER

(to Rachel)

Will you be coming home for the Sabbath?

RACHEL

No, Papa, I won't be coming home.

> (Rachel and Steven exit. Hannah
> enters with Karl Jaspers, a large,
> friendly man in his 40's who sits at his
> desk)

Scene 17 Karl Jasper's office

JASPERS

(Perusing papers in a folder)

Everything is in order, Fraulein Arendt. I see you spent a summer semester with Husserl at Freiburg before coming here.

HANNAH

Yes. Professor Heidegger speaks highly of him.

JASPERS

Professor Heidegger speaks highly of you!

HANNAH

What did he say about me?

JASPERS

(He takes a letter from the folder and reads)

'Hannah is one of my best students. With dedication to the discipline, and sufficient patience, she is destined for greatness.'

HANNAH

Too much praise embarrasses as does too little. I'm grateful for his recommendation, but philosophic greatness is not what I'm aiming for right now. I need a little time off from Professor Heidegger and his way of thinking.

JASPERS

Have you something in mind for your doctoral work?

HANNAH

There are signs that we Germans are becoming more cohesive, but some of our people are being maligned and socially rejected.

JASPERS

You are referring to the increase in anti-Semitism?

HANNAH

Yes.

JASPERS

Are you thinking a little dose of Christian ethics will help?

HANNAH

Two thousand years of Christian ethics have not helped Jews.

JASPERS

We need a major voice to speak up and remind us.

HANNAH

What about St. Augustine? His notion of love. He has some interesting things to say about loving one's neighbor.

JASPERS

Are you asking if I will supervise your dissertation on that topic?

HANNAH

(Nodding)

If you think it a proper topic and if you'll have me.

JASPERS

We must talk more about St. Augustine, but of course I'll be glad to supervise your work. Tell me about my good friend, Professor Heidegger. Did you find him exciting?

HANNAH

Yes, but it wasn't easy being his student. He required a great deal of me. More than I could willingly give.

JASPERS

You decided to leave Marburg because the work was too burdensome?

HANNAH

No, work has never been a problem for me. I made a decision to leave. Professor Heidegger said that he would recommend me to you for my doctoral work. I accepted his suggestion.

JASPERS

Welcome to Heidelberg. My wife, Gertrud, and I would be delighted to have you to lunch. Tomorrow, if you can make it.

HANNAH

(Nodding)

I would like that very much. Thank you.

JASPERS

We'll see you at 2.

> (Hannah crosses to center, puts on a
> raincoat and waits at a rail-stop.
> Heidegger in hat and coat crosses to
> meet her)

Scene 18 Railway station

HEIDEGGER

I knew you would come if you got my message. I am free
for the weekend.

HANNAH

When it's over, how will I be able to leave you without
feeling great pain?

HEIDEGGER

Just be happy we're together, now. We'll go to the inn.
Come.

> (He takes her hand, leads her away)

> (Hannah, in Jasper's office, sits with
> her feet up on a table, reading a
> newspaper; lowers it when Jaspers

enters)

Scene 19 Jasper's office

JASPERS

I'm glad you feel free to make yourself comfortable after a year of hard labor with me.

HANNAH

(Ignoring his remark, puts her feet down) Rosenberg has written another scurrilous article in *The People's Observer*. He has divided our world into Aryans and non-Aryans. The mythical Aryans, he says, are the ancestors of Germans and the superior race.

JASPERS

You feel uneasy?

HANNAH

You know I do. And so does Gertrud.

JASPERS

I say to you, as I say to her, Reason will prevail. The Greeks discovered Reason, but Reason's home is here, in Germany, the land of Goethe, Kant and Hegel.

HANNAH

And Heidegger?

JASPERS

I just finished reading Being and Time. Heidegger has forsaken Reason, and from the inwardness of his own solitude, he's trying to get in touch with Being itself.

HANNAH

If it can be done, he will do it.

JASPERS

I wonder.

HANNAH

I don't.

JASPERS

His followers are waiting for instructions. He alone writes the rules of Being's movements, its comings and goings.

HANNAH

Like his followers, we must wait and see. He isn't harming anyone.

JASPERS

Do philosophers EVER harm anyone?

HANNAH

Only one has been found guilty of it.

JASPERS

You know very well that Socrates was innocent of corrupting the youth.

HANNAH

How can philosophy progress if students are not corrupted?

JASPERS

Don't be cynical.

HANNAH

If philosophers harm their students, how might they do it?

JASPERS

By weaving a web of Unreality so persuasively that students are drawn into it, losing their desire to be critical.

HANNAH

Let students beware!

JASPERS

Learning is a hazardous business.

HANNAH

Especially for the young!

> (Martial music is heard; they both listen as it increases; Hannah goes to the window)

Professor! Look! The Brown Shirts are in town, again! We'll be treated to more of their hateful lies!

> (Martial music and beer-drinking songs are clearly heard.)

JASPERS

> (Looks out the window with Hannah.)

They must be on their way to Munich. Stay indoors. Hitler has been warned. He'll be jailed again if he allows his thugs to go too far.

HANNAH

If that man ever comes to power, I and some others will be in serious trouble!

JASPERS

Hitler will never come to power. Germans are a people of Reason and Culture.

HANNAH

Listen to what those men are saying.

(Sounds of voices chanting: Juden, heraus!)

They are not people of Reason!

JASPERS

They don't represent us! The very essence of a German is Rationality and Humanity!

HANNAH

You're defining YOURSELF!

JASPERS

I'm sorry, Hannah.

HANNAH

Don't pity me for who I am!

JASPERS

I'm saddened that you're experiencing these difficulties. You're GERMAN, too, and you mustn't forget it.

> (We hear Hitler's voice on the radio
> and Germans cheering. There is
> military music and deafening beer-
> drinking songs of German men.)

> (Lights up on Rachel and Steven)

Scene 20 Center stage

RACHEL

I'm sorry my Father behaved as he did, Steven, and I apologize. But you failed me. You failed both of us.

STEVEN

I'm sorry, too. I'm really very, very sorry. I told you I don't like deception.

RACHEL

What about undermining your own cause? What about me?

STEVEN

You're right. I was momentarily confused, I felt pressed. Maybe I can fix things.

RACHEL

There is nothing you can do right now.

(Pause)

But my Father did get to you, didn't he?

STEVEN

I was rejected! He knows who he is, who you are, and who I am not.

RACHEL

If you'd been told who you are from the moment of your birth, you would have an identity, too!

STEVEN

Are you knocking "plain American?"

RACHEL

It's not an identity.

STEVEN

It suits my way of thinking! It's a parsimonious way of looking at myself and other actual things. No metaphysics! And you don't have to live in America to be thoughtfully plain. After all, most Americans aren't plain.

RACHEL

I sometimes wish I were plain. My Jewishness is with me all the time. I FEEL it as a Presence.

STEVEN

You aren't religious any more.

RACHEL

No, but I'm tied to a Being which is Jewish. It's not Race. It's not Religion. It's not exactly Ethnicity or Culture or rites and rituals. It's deeper. Do you see my difference as an obstacle?

STEVEN

Don't be silly.

RACHEL

Then you wouldn't want me to change who I am!

STEVEN

I don't want you to change at all!

RACHEL

But I AM changing, and it's YOUR fault!

STEVEN

My fault? Rachel, I'm not a philosopher, but if your tie to Being is important to you, keep it. I can live with that.

RACHEL

You make Being sound like something a person wears. Something that can be pulled on or cast off!

STEVEN

You seem to be looking for something to hold on to. I'm making myself available, but 'you're looking beyond me. Is Martin Heidegger offering you his hand? Is that it?

RACHEL

Yes.

STEVEN

Are you sure you can trust him?

RACHEL

I have no other choice at the moment. My personal identity
is somehow tied to a Being. inside my brain! It's as simple,
or complex, as that.

(Turns to Hannah and Jaspers)

HANNAH

(Hannah speaks the letter which Jaspers
holds in his hand.)

'Dear Professor Jaspers: Nazi propaganda has affected life in
Berlin. It has changed the consciousness of Berliners. Their
eyes tell me I'm not welcome. Their eyes tell me I'm a Jew. I
feel the burden of my countrymen's contempt and hate. I
need a little philosophic consolation. Please write. Your
loyal student, Hannah.'

JASPERS

'Dear Hannah: My eyes see you as GERMAN! You were
born in Germany! You are a citizen! You said yourself that
you identify with the German language, with German
philosophy, and with German literature. That makes you

GERMAN! All you need add is OUR historical and political destiny. Be consoled my loyal student, Reason and compassion will win out! Very Sincerely, your professor and friend, Karl Jaspers.'

HANNAH

'My Esteemed Professor: I was arrested and held for 8 days. My mother is fearful for our safety. We may have to leave. France is our likely destination. I won't be sharing YOUR political and historical destiny. The Authorities and my fellow citizens are forcing me to become what they PERCEIVE: a Jew.'

JASPERS

'Dear Hannah: I write not knowing where you are. The National Socialists are striding onto the world stage, as you predicted. Reason is losing ground. Please write.'

> (Freiburg University. A Nazi Official in storm coat and hat carries a lectern with a swastika and places it downstage. He is followed by Heidegger wearing Jodhpurs and boots. The Nazi Official stands to the side. Heidegger addresses the faculty. This is his Rector's Address.)

Scene 21 University lecture hall

HEIDEGGER

Members of the Faculty and honored guests. As Rector of this University I must lead, spiritually and intellectually. All true knowing is philosophy. Only when we submit to the power of the BEGINNING of our spiritual-historical existence can true knowing exist FOR us and THROUGH us. Through Early Greek philosophy and its language BEING is comprehended. Coming to BE, we Germans will have a glorious FATE.

(He crosses to Jaspers at Heidelberg University)

JASPERS

(Holds out his hand to greet Heidegger)

Good to see you, Martin.

(They shake hands)

I was unable to hear you in person, but I thank you for sending me a copy of your Rector's address. My sincere congratulations. You're becoming Hitler's philosophical Fuehrer!

HEIDEGGER

Thank you, Karl. Hitler is moving rapidly. We must run just to keep up with him. Can you believe it! I have a national, perhaps an international, role to play in education...

JASPERS

and politics. You may succeed where Plato failed.

HEIDEGGER

My situation IS mindful of Plato's and his visits to Syracuse isn't it?

JASPERS

Very much so.

HEIDEGGER

But the Tyrant that Plato tried to turn into a philosopher-king was not the man of destiny our Fuehrer is.

JASPERS

But Hitler is uneducated! Do you really think such a crude man can lead the German Nation?

HEIDEGGER

Karl, have you seen those marvelous hands? We must wake up! Hitler is leading us into new POLITICAL Reality. We intellectuals must embrace it. Align our thoughts with it.

JASPERS

My position, as you well know, requires some circumspection. I am a German married to a Jew. I don't belong to The Party. At this very moment here at the University, I'm merely tolerated. You're accepted by The Party. You speak for philosophy. What an opportunity!

HEIDEGGER

I feel it too, Karl. Our Youth and our People can be molded by philosophy.

>(Heidegger walks to the lectern. He addresses an assembly of Pro-Nazi Students. Jaspers, Steven, and Rachel watch)

Students of Heidelberg, I leave you with these few thoughts: The National Socialist Spirit must not be suffocated by humanizing, Christian ideas. Mark my words: A FIERCE BATTLE will be fought. Stand with the STATE! NEW COURAGE, and it alone, will open your eyes to that which is to come.

>(He pauses for emphasis)

Whoever does not survive the battle, lies where he falls. The battle will be fought out of the strengths of the new Reich that Chancellor Hitler will bring into BEING. Remember this: The Fuehrer alone IS the present and future German REALITY and its law. Heil Hitler!

>(The students are wildly enthusiastic. Heidegger is elated. Jaspers is visibly uncomfortable and moves to one side.
>
>Lights up on Rachel and Steven who move forward)

Scene 22 Center stage

STEVEN

Isn't Heidegger saying Hitler himself is Germanic BEING when he asserts that Hitler IS the present and future German REALITY?

RACHEL

That's what Heidegger said.

STEVEN

In other words, the REALITY that is Hitler, German REALITY, and the BEING that Heidegger obsesses over are one and the same thing.

RACHEL

If would seem so.

STEVEN

That makes Heidegger's BEING a totalitarian Metaphysical Entity!

RACHEL

Indeed. If it is politicized.

STEVEN

Didn't Heidegger allow Hitler the honor of giving BEING its political character?

RACHEL

Yes. Heidegger had great hopes for Germany when Hitler came to power.

STEVEN

Permit me a little observation. The BEING you philosophers talk about seems to be just one Grand Empty Bag passed around to be filled as the next metaphysician dictates! Didn't Hegel's Spirit-Bag make a political touch-down in Germany last century?

RACHEL

That's not fair!

STEVEN

Philosophers endow BEING with religious powers, political powers, the power to move history. BEING is given social, ethical, and racial work to do. Makes a fellow wonder about the use and abuses of metaphysics. Are the common folk aware of who and what is pulling and pushing them around?

RACHEL

The common folk are not likely to understand metaphysics. If they ever do, metaphysics might well disappear.

STEVEN

You might want to give them a little help.

RACHEL

Thanks for your insights.

STEVEN

Ok. Where was Hannah when the little magician from Messkirch became a supporter of The Chancellor of Death?

RACHEL

She escaped with her mother to France.

STEVEN

And Jaspers?

RACHEL

He was in Heidelberg. Hitler changed the laws and he was not allowed to teach. He was married to a Jew.

STEVEN

Did the man of Being and the man of Reason meet and talk philosophy during Germany's descent into Hell?

RACHEL

They were on the outs. In 1935 Heidegger wrote Jaspers a letter. He'd resigned as Rector of Freiburg and settled back into teaching. Listen to what Heidegger says.

(As she begins to read, a Nazi Official enters)

'...my work is laborious groping in the dark. I have two great thorns in my flesh--the struggle with the faith of my birth, and failing to connect my Rectorship with my philosophic thinking.'

STEVEN

What do you make of those thorns?

RACHEL

Heidegger was more deeply involved in Christian theology than he imagined. When Hitler appeared, he was suddenly confronted with the need to get a handle on Being-on-the-move, living history, for his Fuehrer.

STEVEN

Hitler's task was easier. He had no problem getting a handle on what you can get a handle on: tanks, aircraft, weapons, and Jews!

RACHEL

Couldn't Heidegger's FAILURE to hitch Being to pull the Nazi Wagon show he is INNOCENT of actively promoting the Nazi political agenda?

STEVEN

Why are you protecting him? Heidegger entered Nazi politics gladly. He was aware that his philosophy of BEING would fit Hitler's purposes to a tee! The question was, would he, Heidegger, be in control of the Movement. For him to believe he COULD be in control shows the utter UNREALITY of the man! Imagine this, Rachel:

> (Heidegger goes to a chair opposite a Nazi Official. Note: this could be played by Steven both as Heidegger and the Nazi Official, switching chairs in a comic rendition of the serious.)

Scene 23 Office of Nazi

NAZI OFFICIAL

I am familiar with your work, Professor, and I believe I am sufficiently knowledgeable in philosophy to report our conversation to the Minister as he has requested. First, then, tell me how the Presocratics can be of help to our Fuehrer.

HEIDEGGER

It was they who inquired into Being and comprehended it.

NAZI OFFICIAL

Tell me, how can Being be of help to our Fuehrer?

HEIDEGGER

Knowledge of Being is the highest knowledge humans can attain to!

NAZI OFFICIAL

Does the Fuehrer need that knowledge to fight and win a war?

HEIDEGGER

Philosophical knowledge is difficult, but our esteemed Fuehrer should have some understanding of it.

NAZI OFFICIAL

Should he ask you to come and tutor him?

HEIDEGGER

Of course not!

NAZI OFFICIAL

Do YOU have personal knowledge of Being and its ways?

HEIDEGGER

In understanding the Presocratics, their language and their special use of terms, I am approaching closer to grasping...

NAZI OFFICIAL

But you don't yet have a personal GRASP on Being Itself?

HEIDEGGER

I believe I am approaching the clearing where...

NAZI OFFICIAL

Professor Heidegger, people are laughing at you.

HEIDEGGER

(Taken aback)

Which people?

NAZI OFFICIAL

Educated people at the Ministry of Education.

HEIDEGGER

(Shocked and embarrassed)

What do they say about me?

NAZI OFFICIAL

They say the man who would be the Fuehrer's philosopher is quite incomprehensible. No one can even guess how Being, whatever that is, can be of any relevance to the Fuehrer's aims and goals for the Third Reich.

HEIDEGGER

(Realizing the official's aim was to humiliate

him)

Philosophy's a solitary undertaking. It's THINKING, itself, and that can't be transferred from one head to another.

NAZI OFFICIAL

Rector Heidegger, the Minister wants your resignation. If you comply, you'll become famous, again, among those who are your devoted followers. If you refuse, you'll become, and forgive me for saying it, the first German philosopher to drink hemlock.

RACHEL

You are asking me to believe that Heidegger delivered Being into Hitler's hands!

STEVEN

He WANTED to! He did the best he could to bring it about.

RACHEL

You don't understand his contribution to philosophy.

STEVEN

What did he do that was so great?

RACHEL

He gave philosophy an entirely new turn.

STEVEN

What turn?

RACHEL

The turn to human existence in this world, anticipating our own death.

STEVEN

Is that news? Sounds morbid.

RACHEL

Deep thinkers demand and merit our trust.

STEVEN

Demand? Don't they have to EARN our trust? Who runs off with a SEER who looks inside himself and yells Eureka I've found Me!

RACHEL

Steven, that's unfair! The ME he found was AUTHENTIC!

STEVEN
Who said his ME was authentic?

RACHEL

Heidegger did.

STEVEN

Give me a break! You would hand your brain over to a guy who validates his own authenticity?

RACHEL

Steven, philosophy depends on the PERSONAL insights of great men. I'm philosophically loyal to Martin Heidegger's project, just as you are loyal to Darwin's. You refuse to see it, but Being IS what we are all about!

STEVEN

Being is obviously YOUR thing.

RACHEL

Yes, and you know why!

STEVEN

Yes, Rachel, I do. Tell me, honestly, are you clear about all that?

RACHEL

Yes and No. I've got to get back to work.

STEVEN

(Not moving)

After the Fuehrer's educational Fuehrer resigned his job as Rector of Freiberg University, and Hannah went to France, what happened to her?

RACHEL

She joined the Zionist movement, helped young Jews go to Palestine, and became a political journalist.

STEVEN

She gave up philosophy?

RACHEL

Not at all. Political philosophy became her focus.

STEVEN

She forgot about her philosopher?

>   (Hannah, looking harried and bedraggled
>   moves front and center)

RACHEL

Listen to the letters she NEVER sent.

HANNAH

>   (She reads a letter she has just finished; she
>   begins in German: the lines from Rilke's
>   poem, then says it in English)

Wehr wenn ich schrie, horte mich aus dem... Who if I cried

out would hear me from among the angels...

(Pause, shakes her head despairingly, almost sobbing)

RACHEL

December, 1934.

HANNAH

'My Dearest Martin. I must write and tell you how I feel, even though my letter will never reach you. The risk for you is too great. I love you, as I have the very first day. You know this, and I have always known this. With God's will, I'll love you more after death. I kiss your brow and your eyes.'

(Long Pause: (Radio Speech of the invasion of Poland)

RACHEL

August, 1939.

HANNAH

'My dearest Martin. The world will never be the same. The road you showed me is longer and more difficult than I imagined. It will take up a whole, long life. Still, it is my only possibility to live. I would lose even my right to live if I should lose my love for you. Please think of me. Your Hannah.'

(Long Pause: Radio Speech: France
surrenders)

RACHEL

May, 1941.

HANNAH

'My dearest Martin. With the help of an American, Varian
Fry, we made it out of France, into Spain, and on to
Portugal. We sail for America tomorrow. We will be
separated by a wide, wide ocean. Since I think of you
always, you are close to me, now and forever. Your
Hannah.'

(Long Pause: Visuals of The Camps;
especially a blow-up of the photo in
Goldhagen of naked women carrying
babies and German soldiers with
rifles. Silence. Dark stage. Silent
visuals indicating the War's end)

HANNAH

'Dear professor Jaspers. I was overjoyed to learn that you
and Gertrud survived the
rise and fall of the Reich. Mailed a package this morning.
More will follow. Tell me what you need: food, clothing,
medicines. I am, as always, your loyal student, Hannah in
America.'

JASPERS

'What wonderful things we received from our Hannah in America! We thank you. More than anything, I thank you for your personal loyalty and your natural humanity. My eyes fill with tears at so rare a spirit as yours.'

HANNAH

'Dear Karl and Gertrud. In the last package, I put in a kosher wurst. If you like it, I'll send more.'

JASPERS

'My Hannah in America. The wurst was excellent. Not the same as German wurst, but tasty nonetheless.'

HANNAH

'Dear Karl and Gertrud. I'm sending you some bacon. Cook it this way: put the slices in a moderately hot pan and fry them over a low flame. Keep pouring the fat off until the slices are crisp.'

JASPERS

'Frying the bacon was a new experience for Gertrud. I found it delicious. She abstained.'

HANNAH

'There will be a few of my essays in the bottom of the next package. Give me your opinion. Do you need vitamins? Dried fruit? Coffee?'

JASPERS

'Dear Hannah. I read your essay on German guilt. Do you really believe that what the Nazis did cannot be comprehended as "crime?"'

HANNAH

'Dear Karl: What the Germans did to Jews goes beyond any definition of "crime!" Crime is mundane. Killing on such a scale and for such a purpose is incomprehensible!'

JASPERS

'Dear Hannah: A guilt that goes beyond all criminal guilt takes on satanic greatness. What the Nazis did was totally BANAL, like bacteria that cause epidemics which kill thousands.'

HANNAH

'My Esteemed Professor. What can you tell me about Martin Heidegger? I've heard mostly rumors about his behavior, but I believe some of them may be true. I haven't made up my mind whether I should ever see him again.'

JASPERS

'Dear Hannah. Heidegger has a lot of explaining to do, and he is very good at that. He may lose his job if his appeal to the Denatzification Commission is turned down. I might consider forgiving him, but Gertrud will not.'

HANNAH

'Dear Karl. I'll be able to see you at last! I'm coming to Europe on a special assignment to recover the remnants of Jewish cultural treasures. Haven't decided whether or not to visit Heidegger. His behavior in regard to Husserl was criminal!'

(Lights up on Rachel and her father)

Scene 24 Rachel's room

RACHEL

(Holding up some sheets)

I said you could read and edit. I didn't ask you to write in your comments!

FATHER

(Hands her all the sheets)

My dear Ruchele, how good to see that you are having second thoughts about your philosopher's mishuganah Being!

RACHEL

Just read what I have written, and tell me about the FORM and GRAMMAR! You can keep your remarks about BEING to yourself.

(Hannah and Heidegger prepare to

meet. They talk aloud to themselves,
nervously arranging their hair,
clothing, etc.)

FATHER

Too bad they didn't hang him, along with Alfred Rosenberg
and the others! Hannah-the-German seems to have turned
against the Zionists.

RACHEL

There were disagreements. She never opposed a homeland
for Jews! The question for her was how Jews and
Palestinians could best get along, and that meant working
out things for themselves.

(We see Hannah in her hotel room in
Freiburg waiting for Heidegger who
is outside the room. Both are very
Nervous; both are visibly older)

HANNAH

(Looks in the mirror, brushes her hair,
arranges clothes; talks to the mirror)

The years have not treated you fairly, Hannachen. A little
make-up here, there. Oh,
God, I need a little make-up everywhere. Martin, do you
remember? Do you remember? We loved one another.

HEIDEGGER

(Also looking in a mirror, in the hall outside
Hannah's room)

Hannah, Hannah. You were the passion of my life. You
were the passion of my life.

(Knocks, waits)

HANNAH

Come in!

(Heidegger opens the door and takes a few
steps inside)

Come in, Martin. Close the door.

(He does so and stands sheepishly)

Let me look at you. Seventeen long and terrible years.

(They examine one another for a few
seconds.)

Shall we be kind, admit we've changed, and forego
comments?

HEIDEGGER

You're home at last.

HANNAH

Home?

HEIDEGGER

Hannah, you were the joy of my life. Looking at you
reminds me that some things
will never change.

HANNAH

I'll take that as a compliment. It sounds quite sincere.

HEIDEGGER

I mean it to be.

HANNAH

You look worried.

HEIDEGGER

I've had some health problems.

HANNAH

You must have suffered. But not as much as some others.
Are you alright now?

HEIDEGGER

I'm well enough to continue my work, if I'm allowed to.

HANNAH

Jaspers, whom I saw in Basel, told me you were in trouble

with the denazification authorities.

HEIDEGGER

They've made false accusations. Jaspers discredited me.
They want to keep me from teaching.

HANNAH

You were an extraordinary teacher, Martin. I can't believe
they would keep you out of the classroom. What are their
accusations?

HEIDEGGER

That I was an active member of the Party, that I'm an anti-
Semite, that I'm not fit to teach our young people. I'm sure
you've seen a copy of the report.

HANNAH

Yes, I have it. Did you corrupt the youth, Martin?

HEIDEGGER

Of course not!

HANNAH

Did you turn away from the traditional democratic gods of
our state and offer up One God for the Folk to worship?

HEIDEGGER

Please, Hannah, you're making light of a very serious matter.

HANNAH

Forgive me, Martin, I'm a little nervous. I'm trying to be light-hearted now. I have some very serious questions to put to you, later.

HEIDEGGER

(With unexpected sharpness)

Put them to me now!

HANNAH

I guess the niceties are over. Are you feeling guilty, Martin?

HEIDEGGER

I feel no guilt!

HANNAH

None?

HEIDEGGER

Absolutely none! Will you hold me guilty for making what even you know was simply an error in judgment back in 1933? I'm a philosopher, not a politician!

HANNAH

You obviously believe you should be held to a different standard than Goebels, Himmler, Rosenberg.

HEIDEGGER

Hannah, have you lost your ability to understand?

HANNAH

I hope not. I assure you I've not lost my desire to believe you.

HEIDEGGER

That's all I ask. That you believe me.

HANNAH

(She walks nervously; he follows and tries to get closer to her.)

You were a famous philosopher in 1933. With your Rector's address, Martin, you put yourself in Hitler's camp. You sold yourself and the University to National Socialism.

HEIDEGGER

I became Rector to defend the University from political interference!

HANNAH

Martin, don't make an error by misjudging my ability to

understand what you did!

HEIDEGGER

I defended the University's right to self-governance! How could I have known what was coming? Did YOU know what was coming and how it would end?

HANNAH

You were an outstanding intellectual, and you were not teaching in a cave! Even if you didn't know what was coming, when it DID come, did you do anything about it?

HEIDEGGER

You don't understand. They were watching us all the time. Our very lives were at stake.

> (He approaches and places his hands on her shoulders; she twists and turns away.)

HANNAH

Did you stop going to Jasper's house because his wife was a Jew?

HEIDEGGER

> (Trying to approach her again)

Certainly not! I knew Gertrude was a Jew. It was just that I had other things to do.

HANNAH

Edmund Husserl was a Jew. He was your professor. He
believed in you, got you his chair in Philosophy.

HEIDEGGER

He was a friend.

HANNAH

Friend? In 1927, you dedicated your great work, Being and
Time, to him! In 1935, Martin, when the second edition came
out, you withdrew your dedication.

HEIDEGGER

Do you know what would have happened to me, and to
Elfrida and our sons, if I hadn't withdrawn that dedication?

HANNAH

When he was old and sick and hospitalized, you didn't visit
him.

HEIDEGGER

I wasn't informed that he was ill.

HANNAH

He was an emeritus member of your faculty! You barred
him from the university!

HEIDEGGER

I didn't! A new law was promulgated. Jews were barred from teaching and from using the facilities. I had to post the announcement.

HANNAH

When he died, you didn't attend his funeral!

HEIDEGGER

How could I!

HANNAH

You failed him because HE WAS A JEW!

HEIDEGGER

Hannah, look at me. I'm innocent.

HANNAH

> (Shaking with anger, she looks squarely into his eyes.)

You refused to work with Jewish students in philosophy.

HEIDEGGER

Who told you that?

HANNAH

I'm so upset I can hardly breathe.

                    HEIDEGGER

          (Reaches out to place his hand on her brow.)

You're working yourself up, unnecessarily, Hannah.

               (Unties her scarf)

There. Is that better.

                    HANNAH

               (Walks nervously)

I've spent many sleepless nights wondering what I would say to you.

                    HEIDEGGER

I can explain. Believe me.

          (Moves closer to her, but she walks away)

                    HANNAH

Your Jewish students...

                    HEIDEGGER

Hannah, they stopped coming!

HANNAH

You turned them away! They needed your help!

HEIDEGGER

The University was changing!

HANNAH

You put your University in Hitler's dirty little hands!

> (Hot and uncomfortable, she loosens her scarf and wipes her brow)

HEIDEGGER

Are you warm, Hannah?

HANNAH

Yes, Martin, I can hardly breathe.

HEIDEGGER

Here, let me...

> (Removes her jacket; she is hardly aware of what he is doing.)

I wanted to protect my University from falling into the wrong hands.

HANNAH

You helped cleanse the faculty of Jews. Were there really too many Jews in the Medical Department?

HEIDEGGER

How did you get that information!

(Begins to unbutton her blouse)

HANNAH

Did you get rid of your own assistant because he was a Jew!

HEIDEGGER

I helped Brock get a job in England. I gave have him the very best recommendation!

HANNAH

Of course, Martin. Give THEM your best recommendation and send them elsewhere! Send them to Jaspers, send them to London, send them to Auschwitz!

HEIDEGGER

Stop it, Hannah!

(She is momentarily silent; distraught; he removes her blouse)

HANNAH

(Over-heated, sweating, almost exhausted; he

takes the handkerchief in her hand and uses
it on her forehead; she seems unaware of
what he is doing)

You organized a summer camp for students and herded
them around as if you were a general!

HEIDEGGER

I took command to bring the University into alignment with
the new educational policies.

HANNAH

You began each of your classes with the Nazi Salute!

(She extends her arm at him)

Heil Hitler!

HEIDEGGER

It was a mere formality! It became the custom!

HANNAH

You, who so loved German culture, became a NAZI!

HEIDEGGER

(Manages to unfasten her skirt)

I resigned the Rectorship.

HANNAH

Did you turn in your membership card?

HEIDEGGER

I don't recall. It was long ago.

HANNAH

(As her skirt drops to the floor)

You never turned in your Nazi membership card.

(He removes her bra)

You don't have to answer, Martin. I investigated, and there
is no record of your disassociating yourself from the Party!
I'll never forgive you your lies and deceits!

HEIDEGGER

(Whispering seductively)

Don't believe the rumors my precious Hannah.

HANNAH

(She removes her panties; totally naked)

Martin, you lie!

HEIDEGGER

Remember, Hannah, remember…

HANNAH

(Softer, without conviction)

You deceive!

HEIDEGGER

Just believe me.

HANNAH

(Softer, still)

You betrayed philosophy.

HEIDEGGER

(Whispering and shushing)

There, there.

HANNAH

(Softly, without expecting an answer)

You're an anti-Semite.

HEIDEGGER

(Takes both of her shoulders and shakes her gently)

Hannah, tell me nothing has changed.

(They stare at one another. Fast curtain)

ACT II

Scene 1 Stage area

> (Rachel, witnessing the last scene of
> Act I, is upset with Hannah and
> confronts her center stage)

RACHEL

So, now you are in bed with a Nazi!

HANNAH

My personal life should not concern you! Are you doing
philosophy or writing a novel!

RACHEL

Your personal relationship with Martin Heidegger...

HANNAH

...is none of your business!

> (Hannah turns away, looks at her watch)

Martin is on his way...

> (With emphasis)

He's bringing me a manuscript, not flowers! Goodbye.

RACHEL

Your life is very important to me, Hannah. Please don't turn me away.

Scene 2 Hannah's room

(Heidegger crosses toward Hannah. Rachel crosses to her room)

HANNAH

Hello, Martin.

(He kisses her on the forehead)

Last evening and this morning are a confirmation of a whole life.

(He starts to speak; she places her hand over his mouth)

When I saw you, time suddenly....

HEIDEGGER

(Removes her hand, kisses her fingers)

...began, for us, again.

HANNAH

My impulse to see you mercifully saved me from committing the only truly unforgivable disloyalty. It would have been a tragic mishandling of my life.

> (He holds up her other hand, kissing her fingers)

Had I refused to see you, it would have been out of pride only. Pure, plain, crazy stupidity. It would not have been for any reason.

HEIDEGGER

I knew you would understand. I hope you believe me.

HANNAH

I do.

HEIDEGGER

> (Pause)

I'd like to stay, but Elfrida is waiting.

> (Hannah stiffens)

I brought you the manuscript.

> (Hands her a folder)

I desperately need your help. A university commission wants to take away my right to teach. They want to deny me my pension.

HANNAH

What can I do?

HEIDEGGER

Come to the public square and watch The Denazification of
Professor Martin Heidegger!

(Lowers his head)

Hannah, stand in my defense.

HANNAH

Denazification. How humiliating, Martin.

HEIDEGGER

The process must run its course. Let the world know, in
your quiet way, that I committed no crime! Let them know I
am not political! French intellectuals are on my side. They
are so deeply indebted to me they have good reasons to
protect my reputation.

(Pauses)

Talk to translators in America. Help me get published in the
English-speaking world.

HANNAH

(Holding the folder close to her)

I will, Martin, I will begin as soon as I return to New York. You have my word.

> (She smiles and kisses his forehead; he turns and moves away; Rachel approaches Hannah)

Scene 3 Stage area

RACHEL

You had plenty of reasons to end your relationship with Martin Heidegger!

HANNAH

Are you looking for reasons to end your love affair with him?

RACHEL

I'm finding it difficult to think of Martin Heidegger only intellectually.

HANNAH

I don't even try. Whatever reasons I had to end our relationship turned out to be false. Martin explained everything. The rumors, the slanderous remarks...

RACHEL

Rumors? He joined the Party! He made speeches praising Hitler. There is evidence that he WAS anti-Semitic!

HANNAH

He was misunderstood! He was maligned and vilified for trespasses he did not commit! A great man has suffered intolerably.

RACHEL

Martin Heidegger didn't lift a finger to help you and your Mother get out of Germany!

HANNAH

The risk! Don't you realize the risk? Martin was Rector of a great university. He was under surveillance. He had too much to lose.

RACHEL

You and your Mother had your lives to lose!

HANNAH

Please understand! Martin committed no crime! Even if he were not a great man, he would be deserving of our understanding and compassion.

RACHEL

Close friendship with an internationally-known Jew like

yourself will help to erase the charge of anti-Semitism. Elfrida must be wild with happiness.

HANNAH

You would think so, but she is jealous almost to the point of madness! Martin has been in a depression from the moment the war ended. He had a nervous breakdown. He needs someone who understands how important he is to the intellectual world.

RACHEL

He is apparently important to his wife, too.

HANNAH

I wish Martin were more aware of Elfrida's pernicious influence.

RACHEL

Did he ever tell you he was unhappy all those years with a wife who was, from the beginning, a dedicated, hard-working Nazi?

HANNAH

Martin's recovery is mine as well. I have personal wounds to heal. Martin pushed me out of Marburg. The Nazis pushed me out of Germany.

RACHEL

Did you sleep with Martin to get revenge?

HANNAH

I want Martin back.

RACHEL

Why would you want him back?

HANNAH

So, my emotional life can be whole again.

RACHEL

(Shakes her head)

Life is more difficult than philosophy.

HANNAH

Is that a remark about your life or mine?

(Rachel lowers and shakes her head)

RACHEL

Mine.

(Pauses)

You could have brought Martin Heidegger down.

HANNAH

Loyalty is a way of living too.

RACHEL

But shouldn't we be free, first, and then choose our
loyalties?

HANNAH

Life doesn't always allow us to proceed in that fashion.

RACHEL

But if we CAN, shouldn't we?

HANNAH

Of course.

RACHEL

You maintained your loyalties and also entered the political
world to help Jews.

HANNAH

I could not do otherwise. Want to know the truth?

RACHEL

Yes.

HANNAH

I would rather have stayed in Germany and become an unknown woman teaching philosophy in a university.

RACHEL

You did not have that option.

HANNAH

The Nazis made me a Jew.

RACHEL

The Nazis made you a Jew? How strange that sounds.

HANNAH

You may have to decide whether you'll be in or out of the tribe, Rachel.

RACHEL

I'm IN, Hannah, but I don't want my life dominated by men and their tribal ways.

HANNAH

If you are IN, Rachel, your Father and the Tribe have God-given rights!

RACHEL

Ok, my Father has rights! And I HAVE RIGHTS!

(Hannah waits for her to calm down)

How could you become your own person and still remain a Jew?

HANNAH

I have always been my own person. I once told Jaspers that if we choose to, each of us should be able to decide who we would like to be, German or Jew or whatever, by just thinking and acting accordingly.

RACHEL

We can CHOOSE our identity?

HANNAH

Who we choose to be is the one great, free choice a person can make.

RACHEL

I'm beginning to understand that choosing NEVER to BE is the more moral choice humans can make.

HANNAH

Are you trying to eliminate Metaphysics? And Religion?

RACHEL

I'm seriously considering it.

HANNAH

Whether you choose to Be, or never to Be, there are consequences.

RACHEL

And opportunities. I feel there is life beyond Being.

> (Hannah nods assent as Rachel crosses to her room)

Scene 4 Hannah's room

HEIDEGGER

(Turns to face Hannah)

Be especially careful about whom you select to translate my manuscript.

HANNAH

I will, Martin.

HEIDEGGER

Send me a draft immediately so I can let someone here in Germany advise me. Go over the translation carefully.

HANNAH

I will do as you say. The publisher is the best I know of and wants you on his list. I'm sending some pages of translations. Tell me if you approve.

HEIDEGGER

Elfrida and I need money. Please tell us how much my manuscript, Being and Time, will bring in the American market. We know nothing about money. You know, so please advise us.

HANNAH

Martin, Jews aren't the only ones who know about money.

HEIDEGGER

(Momentarily embarrassed)

No, of course not.

(Rachel crosses to Hannah, Heidegger crosses to his office)

Scene 5 Stage area

RACHEL

What remains to be done for Martin Heidegger?

HANNAH

(Looks at Heidegger admiringly)

His reputation is secure. Three major works are now published.

RACHEL

You worked tirelessly on his behalf.

HANNAH

That shouldn't surprise you.

(Again, looks at Heidegger)

Great men are rare beings.

RACHEL

What about great women?

HEIDEGGER

(Impatient, interrupts)

Hannah! Are you two chattering in my presence?

RACHEL

(Indignant, turns to Hannah)

You were saying great men are rare. And great women?

HANNAH

(Looking at Heidegger)

Without Being they are invisible.

RACHEL

Professor Heidegger, did you celebrate Hannah's works?

HEIDEGGER

Her works?

RACHEL

Yes. What is your opinion of her book, On Totalitarianism?

HEIDEGGER

It's in English! I don't read English!

HANNAH

It was translated into German, Martin.

(To Rachel)

The truth is, Martin is always occupied with his thinking.

RACHEL

(To Heidegger)

Are you aware of all that Hannah wrote? The prizes she
won? The honors bestowed on her?

(Heidegger remains silent)

HANNAH

(Ironic)

Martin's genius REQUIRES him to ignore me and the
World!

(Looks at Heidegger)

RACHEL

(To Hannah)

I can't believe you're willing to be ignored!

HANNAH

It's the small price I pay...

HEIDEGGER

(Objects to their talk; addresses Rachel)

One question. In this work you are doing, will you treat me
fairly?

RACHEL

I have an intellectual responsibility to tell the truth.

HEIDEGGER

Good. Then we can begin. My professional life is coming to an end. What would you like to know?

RACHEL

Why you never said one word about the six million?

(Holds up her hand)

Wait. I mustn't put it that way. See what I did? I spoke of living flesh and blood individuals--men, women, children, babies, born and unborn--as if they were all ONE DEATH in ONE MOMENT of history.

(She is too emotional to continue)

HEIDEGGER

Perhaps you would like to ask me another question.

RACHEL

No. Why have you remained silent all these years?

HEIDEGGER

(Lowers and shakes his head)

Have you another question?

RACHEL

Why have you never admitted any guilt for the actions of Adolph Hitler whom you supported?

HEIDEGGER

(Lowers his head and waits)

Have you a question about philosophy?

RACHEL

You prefer to remain silent.

HEIDEGGER

Except on the sacred ground that is philosophy.

RACHEL

That's very risky, for me.

(Pauses, thoughtfully)

Nietzsche has remarked about the ERROR of Being and its power of persuasion.

HEIDEGGER

He's wrong that Being is an error in our thinking.

RACHEL

Even I feel its persuasion.

HEIDEGGER

Through whose efforts?

RACHEL

My Father's, but also yours.

HEIDEGGER

Tell me.

RACHEL

As with you, Being envelops my deepest feelings of who I am and who my people are. It gives us a sort of...metaphysical...permanence and continuity.

HEIDEGGER

Don't be arrogant. Being giveth of itself and Being taketh away.

RACHEL

Is it, perhaps, you, Professor Heidegger, who giveth Being and can taketh it away?

HEIDEGGER

(Gives her a cutting glance)

It is Being's choice.

RACHEL

So, the Jews could exist, without Being, and not even know it.

HEIDEGGER

Being took a turn through another people.

RACHEL

The German people.

(Heidegger nods)

Wouldn't you say Being let the German people down?

HEIDEGGER

(With unexpected anger)

THEY LET BEING DOWN! They did not rise to the greatness Being expected of them! The German People LET ME DOWN!

(Rachel is shocked)

RACHEL

Your Fuehrer, in his bunker in Berlin, must have had those same thoughts and feelings.

(He glares at her)

Professor Heidegger, I don't fully understand you and Being.

HEIDEGGER

No, of course you don't. Being has withdrawn into oblivion. Being is no longer interested in human history. It is no longer acting behind the backs of men.

RACHEL

(After a pause)

You seem to be saying that Being is pissed at us.

HEIDEGGER

What does it mean, "pissed"?

RACHEL

I mean, like you, Being must be angry and upset. Should we draw any interesting conclusion from the fact that you and BEING are withdrawing into oblivion at the same time?

HEIDEGGER

Make whatever inference you wish. Being and I are immune to logic.

RACHEL

If BEING has gone bye bye, you are without a job.

HEIDEGGER

Trivializing philosophy comes easily to Americans.

(Pauses)

No matter, my work is done. I'll end my life here in the village of my birth.

RACHEL

You haven't wandered far from where you were born.

(He gestures for Rachel to follow him; they walk)

HEIDEGGER

As with Emannuel Kant, I stayed close to home. My father was Sexton in the church here in Messkirch.

(Now, as if in the church)

As a child, I rang the bells, I played in the yard of this church with my brother, Fritz. We helped the Holy Father on Sundays.

(He pauses, a bit choked with his memories)

I've made arrangements for a church funeral. Something simple. A few words at the grave. Perhaps these: he was born, he worked hard, and he died.

RACHEL

A world-famous philosopher put to rest with words fit for a peasant! Some would like to hear words which would make all the difference, if you allow them to be spoken.

HEIDEGGER

What words?

RACHEL

Martin Heidegger, the most profound philosopher of the 20th century is returning to his native soil. He wandered Godless through the thicket of philosophy, but returned before the end to The Church of his youth.

HEIDEGGER

My gravestone is to have no cross!

(Indicating with his hands)

This is a simple, but beautiful church, isn't it? Listen.

(Organ music, boys' choir ethereal voices in song)

Do you hear it?

RACHEL

Yes.

HEIDEGGER

(Overcome by his own thoughts; in a semi-
trance; softly)

Do you feel something?

RACHEL

(Listens intently)

What is it?

HEIDEGGER

(Softly)

Something spiritual. Meister Eckhart. His presence seems to
hover about us.

RACHEL

(Softly)

Is he speaking to you, Professor Heidegger?

HEIDEGGER

Eckhart is The Church's greatest mystic. He's German, you
know. It's such an honor to be in his presence.

RACHEL

I understand.

HEIDEGGER

(Coming to his senses)

Are you listening, Rachel?

RACHEL

Yes, I'm listening.

(She allows him time to get himself together)

Professor Heidegger, do you realize how difficult all this is for me?

HEIDEGGER

What is difficult, Rachel?

RACHEL

I am trying to KNOW for myself! You're not helping me!

HEIDEGGER

Knowing is a leap YOU must make! Do you understand what I am saying?

RACHEL

Yes.

HEIDEGGER

Hopefully you'll progress beyond that.

RACHEL

My head is spinning!

(Pauses)

Do you remember the young Hannah? She appeared suddenly one morning in your classroom...

HEIDEGGER

...wearing a green dress. A bright ribbon tied her shiny black hair in the back.

RACHEL

She was striking.

HEIDEGGER

Enchanting. Exotic. The essence of maidenly Jewishness.

RACHEL

That's what attracted you, her being a Jew?

HEIDEGGER

Of course. Would she have denied it?

RACHEL

For the love of her life, I'm sure she would not.

(Heidegger pulls himself out of his reverie)

HEIDEGGER

Come outside.

(They walk, as if outside; he indicates)

The Black Forest and the mountains are my home. Look.
Look around. Hiking is my great pleasure.

RACHEL

A friend of yours reported that on hikes with him, when
you came upon a church or chapel, you dipped your finger
in the stoup and genuflected. Is that true?

HEIDEGGER

Indeed, it is. Churches are historical places. Where there has
been so much praying, there the divine is present in a very
special way.

RACHEL

You FELT the presence of the divine on those occasions?

HEIDEGGER

Its closeness.

RACHEL

You genuflected?

(He nods, smiling)

The religion of your youth is still with you!

HEIDEGGER

It's a thorn I bear.

RACHEL

How could you!

(He is shocked)

You deceived all of us!

HEIDEGGER

(Becoming angry)

If you are deceived, Rachel, you do it to yourself! Thanks to
Martin Heidegger, Being's character is revealed at last. It is
Time Itself! Manifested as Human Personal and Collective
History. To you and Nietzsche, Being may seem like a
vapor, almost like nothing, but it is not. Do you understand?

RACHEL

(Looks directly at him)

Yes, I understand, I actually do.

(She turns and goes to Hannah)

Scene 6 Stage area

HANNAH

You look wretched, Rachel. What's the matter?

RACHEL

Philosophy is crumbling under my feet.

HANNAH

Don't believe everything The Philosopher says.

RACHEL

You did!

HANNAH

(Taken aback)

You're angry with me, Rachel.

RACHEL

I'm angry with EVERYBODY! Hannah, I'm losing all I
hoped to hold together in my life!

HANNAH

(Holds her close, briefly)

What can you do?

RACHEL

Drive a stake through Martin Heidegger's deceitful heart.

(Hannah is shocked. Heidegger approaches Jaspers on the side)

HEIDEGGER

Beware of that young philosopher. I don't trust her.

Scene 7 Rachel's room

(Rachel's Father approaches Rachel)

FATHER

(His hat in his hand; affecting a solemn and sad appearance)

Forgive me, Rachel. I realize you have your work, but I must speak to you.

RACHEL

What is it, Papa?

FATHER

Steven dropped by my office, just to say hello, but I felt he wanted to talk. I didn't. He's a good man, but not for you.

(She turns and throws up her hands)

Steven is not my main concern. It's you I'm concerned about.

RACHEL

You've learned something about me that disturbs you?

FATHER

You've given up all outward signs of Being who you Are. You seem totally uninterested in the Jewish Community, Jewish friends, Jewish affairs, and, sad to say, your Jewish Father. What's left, Rachel, what's inside?

RACHEL

Just me.

FATHER

You seem to be moving away from us.

RACHEL

I'm trying to live a life that's my own.

FATHER

If you are only for yourself, Rachel, WHO are you?

RACHEL

Just me, Papa, your little Ruchele. I still have you, I'll always have Mama, and our people.

FATHER

No, Rachel. No you won't. Our people need someone who is bound to them by the God of our Fathers.

RACHEL

You were right, Papa. I have work to do.

FATHER

What work is more important than being ever mindful of who you are?

RACHEL

I know who I am, Papa. My work is important. For Mama. And for me. I'm trying to UNDERSTAND! You can't do that for me. Forgive me, but I have a trial to conduct.

FATHER

You are conducting a trial?

RACHEL

Yes.

> (She moves front and addresses the audience)

Ladies and gentlemen, Martin Heidegger is guilty of crimes against humanity.

> (She turns and addresses Heidegger and the others)

Professor Heidegger, please take a seat, there.

> (Points; he goes)

Hannah, will you and Professor Jaspers be seated, there?

> (Points; they go)

Papa, stand opposite our philosophers, and you, Steven, stand beside my Father and keep order.

> (They go as directed; after a pause, she turns to face the audience again)

Ladies and gentlemen, Hitler, Himmler, Goebels, Goring and other leaders of the Third Reich are dead. Some committed suicide, some were found guilty and sentenced to death at Nuremberg.

> (Looks at Heidegger)

Martin Heidegger will never face a criminal court. Never in history has anyone guilty of doing metaphysics gone to prison for it.

HANNAH

Rachel, this is absurd! Don't do this!

FATHER

(Steps forward and points at Hannah)

You lost your right to be heard in the Jewish Community when you went soft on Eichmann the Nazi!

RACHEL

Papa, please!

(Steven takes his arm; they step back)

Karl, your reputation as a good and compassionate man is recognized. You and Hannah were practically father and daughter, but both of you were too forgiving of your colleague.

(Indicates Heidegger)

Hannah, you and Karl closed your eyes before and after the war to the extent of Martin Heidegger's involvement with National Socialism. Both of you accepted his lies, fearing the great man would reject you if you offended him.

HANNAH

Rachel, I object!

JASPERS

You are not being fair. What you are doing is not
philosophy!

RACHEL

What I am doing is looking into the heart and mind of a
Great Teacher.

HEIDEGGER

Who are you to judge me!

RACHEL

(Turns half-way to audience and looks at
them)

Philosophers ARE superior people. They're Western
Society's most elite cult. Professor Heidegger, the Cult-
Leader of BEING, not only survived, he prospered.
Members of our family did not survive.

(She looks at her father)

We were all changed forever. My Father was strengthened
in his faith. My Mother lost hers. The God of the Jews, she
said and need I add, the God of Christians and Muslims---
died at Auschwitz.

FATHER

Rachel! Don't!

RACHEL

I've good reason to try to understand the world and you...

(She looks at her father)...and Mama and
Professor Heidegger, too.

(She struggles with words and feelings)

What is prayer for, Mama asks, if not to be answered by a
living and loving God? WHAT IS IT FOR!

FATHER

Rachel, I demand that you stop this!

RACHEL

YOU MUST LISTEN, Papa. You've got to LISTEN! Mama
got it right! God died at Auschwitz. Nietzche's declaration
was premature.

(To Heidegger)

You remember Auschwitz.

HEIDEGGER

I know NOTHING of Auschwitz!

RACHEL

Oh, you do, Professor Heidegger. You do, and you did.

Let me ask the fair-minded Professor Jaspers if he thinks you were endorsing Auschwitz when you opened each of your classes with...

> (She raises her arm and says, loudly)

Sieg Heil!

JASPERS

He was endorsing the system. He is, shall we say, metaphysically guilty.

HEIDEGGER

I'm guilty of nothing!

FATHER

What sort of nonsense are you uttering, Professor Jaspers? Metaphysical guilt? Jews did not die a metaphysical death!

HEIDEGGER

My hands are clean!

> (Raises his arms and shows the palms of his hands)

RACHEL

> (Turns to the audience)

Ladies and gentlemen, what are we to do with that special group of men whose hands become, at worst, metaphysically dirty?

(Pauses)

They are never brought to trial.

HEIDEGGER

Rachel, you're advised to let things be. We must WILL no more. Our speech must offer Being an abode. Here between birth and our own death, we can only wait.

RACHEL

Wait. For yet another metaphysical man to guide us. Wait for him to confer Being on us.

(Shakes her head)

Being. It's the heart of Metaphysics. Such an esoteric subject.

(Looks at Heidegger, who is silent)

Is Metaphysics harmful? Could THAT be the most important question a philosopher can ask?

HEIDEGGER

You're wasting my time.

RACHEL

Being is IMAGINARY! An ILLUSION! Belief in its 'Reality'
is the ultimate Delusion! And so is its Twin...

(She looks at her Father)

The Supernatural!

HEIDEGGER

You blaspheme the wise and holy men of philosophy and
religion!

RACHEL

One wise man characterized Germany as the most
metaphysical of nations. That was you, Professor Heidegger.
Germany, the most metaphysical of Nations. Sounds
innocuous. Romantic. Professor Heidegger refers to a nation
and a people already primed with Aryan myth, a Racist
ideology, and the desire to become what they are told they
can Be.

HEIDEGGER

I did not control political reality in Germany!

RACHEL

You are quite right about that.

HEIDEGGER

It was Hitler, Goebels, Himmler. You wouldn't understand,

but The National Socialist Movement had great promise!

RACHEL

Those words will live in our memory. You declared the Movement had an inner truth and greatness. Only a man of metaphysics could SEE its inner Reality. More than six million others FELT the consequences of that belief.

JASPERS

Rachel, you should not continue this trial without a jury!

RACHEL

We have a Jury.

(Indicates the audience)

HANNAH

I thought we had become friends.

RACHEL

We have.

(Turns to Jaspers)

Professor Jaspers, you knew about Professor Heidegger's teaching early on, but kept it a secret.

JASPERS

I told the Denazification Commission!

RACHEL

We are grateful that you did. Would you mind repeating what you said?

JASPERS

'...Heidegger's mode of thinking...seems to me to be fundamentally unfree, dictatorial and uncommunicative...'

RACHEL

Did you select those words carefully in characterizing professor Heidegger's totalitarian mode of thinking?

JASPERS

Totalitarian?

RACHEL

Yes. You said Heidegger's mode of thinking was fundamentally unfree, dictatorial and uncommunicative. Isn't that some of what we mean by "totalitarian?"

JASPERS

It's authoritarian.

HEIDEGGER

You were paying me back for past grievances of which I am

innocent!

JASPERS

(Addresses Heidegger directly)

I stand by my characterization of your mode of thinking.

HANNAH

He was brilliant in the classroom!

RACHEL

Thanks for supporting the claim of his greatness as a teacher. But, Professor Jaspers, truth-telling requires that you NOT put aside your personal grievances. Please elaborate.

JASPERS

When I was removed as chairman of the philosophy department at Heidelberg...

(He turns to face Heidegger)

...Why Martin, WHY did you not say one word in my defense?

(Heidegger looks away and remains silent)

When The Party banned the publishing of my books, why didn't you protest? Why did you remain silent?

(Heidegger remains silent)

RACHEL

There was nothing politically offensive in your books, Professor Jaspers. You did, however, commit the indefensible act of having married Gertrud. You knew SHE was in danger. Did you also feel you weren't safe?

JASPERS

When I wasn't allowed to teach any more, we made the decision to carry...some pills.

RACHEL

That must have been terribly stressful for both of you.

JASPERS

We waited each night for a knock on the door.

RACHEL

Did you speak with Martin Heidegger about ways of protecting your wife and yourself?

JASPERS

I did not.

RACHEL

Is it because you KNEW Gertrud would receive no help

from him?

(Jaspers remains silent)

Professor Jaspers, please continue reading what you wrote about your colleague to the Denazification Commission.

JASPERS

'...until such time as a genuine rebirth takes place within him, and is SEEN to be at work within him, I think it would be quite wrong to turn such a teacher loose on the young people of today. First of all, the young must be taught to think for themselves.'

RACHEL

(Looking at Jaspers)

Professor Jaspers, wouldn't it be wrong to turn such a teacher loose on young people ON ANY DAY?

JASPERS

Teachers have a responsibility to protect students...

RACHEL

...and not sleep with them? Why didn't you tell someone years ago about Professor Heidegger's mode of thinking, since it was clear to you that he presented a danger to students, not least of all, that they would not learn how to think for themselves?

JASPERS

That is simply never done!

RACHEL

Of course, it isn't!

(Looking at her Father)

What would happen to us if young people learned to think for themselves?

(Addressing Jaspers)

Did a genuine rebirth ever take place within Professor Heidegger, or did anyone ever SEE it to be at work within him?

JASPERS

I never saw it, and there is no record of it.

(He looks at Hannah for comment; she remains silent)

RACHEL

Rebirths are even more miraculous than births.

FATHER

Professor Heidegger's professional resurrection was quite miraculous, but assured, given Professor Arendt's skills in getting his works translated and published. BEING was saved.

HEIDEGGER

(Addressing Rachel's father)

Without the Metaphysics of Being, Judaism is empty rites and rituals!

(The Father looks at Rachel, not knowing how to respond; Steven tries to help him)

STEVEN

(Addressing Heidegger)

Without metaphysics, wouldn't the air be cleared for more sensible and valuable ways of doing philosophy, ways that would be helpful to mankind and even useful to scientists?

HEIDEGGER

Philosophy USEFUL? Philosophy bakes no bread! If mankind wants BREAD, it should go to the bake-shop!

STEVEN

Philosophy bakes PIE, and you know where that is!

(Points UP)

Scientists get no knowledge of the world, and usually only a hard time, from philosophers!

RACHEL

Steven, please!

HEIDEGGER

(To Steven)

Scientists don't THINK! They grind out data, they produce information and manufacture technology. They are ignorant of BEING, even the BEING of the Big Bang!

STEVEN

(Spoken slowly and with emphasis)

Professor Heidegger, the Big Bang came NAKED. It was just Bang. No Being before, during, or after. Physical forces don't need any metaphysical help. The notion of Being is superfluous!

RACHEL

Steven, please.

HEIDEGGER

(To Rachel)

You would like to destroy my work. Fortunately, yours is a small and insignificant voice.

RACHEL

I would like to be free of dangerous and arbitrary authority.

HEIDEGGER

You are free to expose your ignorance.

RACHEL

Or free to tell the truth. Behold, ladies and gentlemen!

(Indicates Heidegger)

In the Absence of Being, our Emperor has...no clothes.

HEIDEGGER

(More confused than angry)

What is she saying?

STEVEN

She's saying BEING IS .... BULLSHIT!

HEIDEGGER

(Holds up his hand to stop Rachel
who tries to proceed; there is a
weighty pause; Jaspers approaches)

Your repeated attempts to humiliate me are unprofessional.
I understand why you're upset. You're a young Jew who is
forcing herself to be something she isn't. In transgressing
your own boundaries, you're trying to free yourself of who

you really are. Is the loss of Being making you feel anxious, guilty, angry?

RACHEL

Detaching myself from a doctrine I once believed in IS making me feel anxious. I will recover. But you will not.

HEIDEGGER

Given who you are and who I AM, Rachel, who, among philosophers, will believe you? Which of us will have the last word?

RACHEL

Last images may be more important than last words. I will remember you retreating into oblivion dragging Being behind you.

HEIDEGGER

If you should feel lonely in your nothingness, Rachel, remember: YOU are the door through which BEING enters the world.

RACHEL

I'm closing the door.

JASPERS

Has the teaching of Metaphysics, then, become a criminal act? Rachel, have you lost sight of the aims and hopes which have inspired Western Civilization!

RACHEL

Isn't it time we questioned our metaphysical and supernatural hopes and aims?

HEIDEGGER

Some men are born to inform mankind and direct it rightly and truly.

RACHEL

Freeing ourselves from the control of metaphysical men is worth striving for.

HEIDEGGER

Are you ready to become the guide for the chaos that is mankind?

RACHEL

No, not at all, but I've given careful thought to your role as self-appointed guide. Through interpretative mystification of Greek texts, you opened a door in the human brain and summoned BEING. You tied Being to our personal and historical sense of TIME. We need to free ourselves of those ties and the hopes they inspire. Steven, would you tell Professor Heidegger what your watch is doing?

(He looks at his watch)

STEVEN

Ticking.

RACHEL

Is it ticking off TIME?

STEVEN

No, like all clocks, it just ticks and the hands move.

RACHEL

Are you saying that TIME has nothing to do with clocks?

STEVEN

That's correct. It has nothing to do with the spinning of the earth, our experience of night and day, or the beating of our hearts. In fact, TIME itself is an illusion.

RACHEL

TIME and BEING. BEING and TIME. What a ghostly pair. Listen.

>   (She points skyward; a ticking sound is
>   heard, increasing in loudness)

BEING is riding into oblivion...on the back of TIME.

>   (The ticking increases in loudness as
>   lights dim. Hannah remains with

Rachel, the others exit)

HANNAH

(Upset)

Is court adjourned for the day?

(Rachel doesn't respond)

Where will you be tomorrow, Rachel?

RACHEL

I don't know. Is there life after metaphysics?

HANNAH`

You seem determined to reduce philosophy to rubble. Kicking up all that emotional dust obscures philosophic vision.

RACHEL

Was Martin Heidegger's vision helpful to you?

HANNAH

His methods were helpful. His vision remains inside his amazingly creative head. Martin is only truly happy when he is talking with himself.

RACHEL

His students thought he was talking to them.

(Pause)

He was really down on the world. Why?

HANNAH

It wasn't going the way he thought it should. And, early on, he came to think that we're all born simply to die.

RACHEL

What a dreadful sentence for the living.

HANNAH

We're not born to die. We're born to begin. The miracles that save the world are the new beginnings that come when individuals know who they are and their babies are born.

RACHEL

Does that include girl babies, too?

(As Hannah moves away, Steven enters)

Scene 8 Stage area

STEVEN

You caused quite a stir.

RACHEL

It had to be done.

STEVEN

Rachel, OUR situation is making me nervous.

RACHEL

I know, Steven, and I'm sorry.

STEVEN

We just keep waiting.

RACHEL

I said I'm sorry.

STEVEN

What are we waiting for?

RACHEL

For me to finish my work.

STEVEN

You look tired.

RACHEL

I need a good night's sleep.

STEVEN

Your work is almost finished.

(She sits with her manuscript and nods)

RACHEL

I have to come to some conclusion about my life.

STEVEN

What then?

RACHEL

Find a way to begin.

STEVEN

Can I help?

RACHEL

(Raising the manuscript)

See me through this dissertation.

STEVEN

(Goes to her, takes the dissertation and looks into her eyes)

Rachel, there is more to your life than these pages. I'm concerned about you. I'm concerned about US! Why must you insist on doing everything yourself? Do you think you can work out your whole life all by yourself? Tell me what I can do. If you don't, I will find a way. Believe me, I will.

RACHEL

Steven, don't do anything crazy. Wait for me. I need to think things through. I'm worried about Papa.

> (Lights dim, then up on Hannah and Martin)

Scene 9 Stage area

HEIDEGGER

It's insulting to have to listen to that young scientist. He's incapable of understanding the roots of his own science and the nature and demands of our German Spirit.

HANNAH

(Rubs his back)

There, there. Does that feel better?

HEIDEGGER

You know it makes me feel better.

HANNAH

I'm preparing a celebration of your birthday. Will that
please you?

HEIDEGGER

I am pleased when we're alone.

HANNAH

Tell me more.

HEIDEGGER

You are the passion of my life.

HANNAH

Do you still desire me?

HEIDEGGER

We made heavenly love on our mountain. There we were
close to the gods.

HANNAH

And the angels.

HEIDEGGER

We have so few opportunities anymore. Still, if you should

cry out, I will hear you. Here, take my hand and we'll go.

> (She takes his hand and allows him to extend
> her arm to go, then stops)

HANNAH

You know Elfrida won't permit you to be alone with me.
But I do believe you are
sincere.

> (She puts his hand on her breast; they start to
> move upstage and stop; he looks at her)

HEIDEGGER

Hannah, I want you to remember this. YOU are the love of
my life.

Scene 10 Stage area

> (Lights dim then up on the Father and
> Steven. Klezmer music is playing. The
> Father does a little dance, Steven
> snaps his fingers.)

STEVEN

May I ask how your change of mind came about? It was so
sudden, a total surprise. I didn't expect it.

FATHER

Necessity, Steven. Rachel was clearly leaning away from the life she's always known. I couldn't let her leave. Jews are not without resources. And sometimes God can find a way. You knocked on my door and our minds found a meeting place.

STEVEN

(Nods)

Our love for Rachel.

FATHER

You felt she wouldn't marry you. I felt that she would! Our solution was made in heaven! It's time for us to be serious. Would you turn off the music?

(Steven does so)

You'll be expected to take part in our community gatherings, regular worship, holiday observances.

STEVEN

If that's what is expected of me, and Rachel wants me too, I'll do it.

FATHER

Rachel was an active member of our Jewish Community before she became...a philosopher. I'm sure she misses the richness of Jewish life. You, Steven, will come in contact with actual Jewish living.

STEVEN

That'll help me build Jewish memories and a usable Jewish past.

FATHER

You'll become historical! And why do you need a growing reservoir of Jewish experiences?

STEVEN

(Guesses)

To make me FEEL Jewish?

FATHER

Those experiences will form the foundation for a secure Jewish IDENTITY. Alright. Good.

> (As the Father pulls a yarmulka from his pocket and places it on Steven's head, Rachel is seen approaching, then stops)

STEVEN

I can't really feel it up there.

> (Puts his hand on his head)

It may fall off.

FATHER

We can pin it on, Steven. Orthodox and Conservative Jewish males wear it in the synagogue, the house, and in the study hall.

STEVEN

This is our study hall.

FATHER

Precisely. Now, as your counselor, I want you to think seriously about the following questions. Take whatever time you need. You must be able to answer "yes" to all of them.

(Begins reading from a sheet of paper)

Do you choose to enter the eternal covenant between God and the People Israel and to become a Jew of your own free will?

STEVEN

I do.

FATHER

Do you...

(Rachel walks toward them)

RACHEL

What is going on here?

STEVEN

We're practicing....

FATHER

We were going to surprise you, Rachel.

RACHEL

Well, you certainly have. In fact, I'm shocked!

FATHER

We didn't want you to know. Until you finished your work.

RACHEL

And then Steven would pop out of a brightly colored box
and announce that he's a Jew?

(Glares at Steven who removes the yarmulka)

What is this?

(Takes the yarmulka from him)

When did you decide to become a Jew, Steven?

STEVEN

You know how much I care for you, Rachel. I couldn't wait

any longer. I couldn't take the risk of your saying no. Your Father found a way to open the door for me.

(Rachel looks at her Father)

RACHEL

You put him up to this?

FATHER

No, Rachel. He asked a question. I had to answer it.

RACHEL

You let him know that he had to become a Jew to have a chance of marrying me?

FATHER

We had a discussion. I pointed in the direction he should take.

RACHEL

Was that the only reason?

FATHER

(Long pause)

God knows, Rachel, I can never allow you to go.

RACHEL

(Takes the sheet of paper from her Father
and, looking at Steven, reads)

Do you pledge your loyalty to Judaism and to the Jewish
people under all circumstances?

STEVEN

(Placing the yarmulka on his head)

I do.

RACHEL

Do you commit yourself to the pursuit of Torah and Jewish
knowledge?

STEVEN

I do.

RACHEL

If we should be blessed with children, do you promise to
raise them as Jews?

STEVEN

(Hesitates; looks at Rachel for guidance)

What should I say?

RACHEL

Say what is in your heart, Steven. Just be honest.

STEVEN

(Looks at the Father)

The question is about more than just us, Dr. Gershon. More than about Rachel and me.

FATHER

Indeed it is, Steven. It's about continuity. A continuity of religious Being since Adam and Eve and the Covenant.

STEVEN

I have no right to bind our children and offer them as gifts to God, Rachel.

RACHEL

You must answer yes to all the questions, Steven. This is the last one.

STEVEN

I can't, Rachel. Dr. Gershon, I owe you an apology, but I meant everything I said. If Rachel wanted it, I could become a Jew....

FATHER

...or a Christian, a Muslim, or a Buddhist. You are

extraordinarily flexible, Steven. I suppose that's an achievement that comes from plainness. You seem to be able to move into and out of religious groups without psychological wear and tear on your soul. I can only be a Jew. Professor Heidegger can only be a German. Rachel wants to choose, but that is not God's way.

(Starts to leave)

RACHEL

Papa?

FATHER

Yes, Rachel.

RACHEL

You refused to see it, but Mama became plain, too.

FATHER

Don't say that to me, Rachel. Don't say that to your Father!

Scene 11 Rachel's room

(Lights down, then focus dimly on Rachel who is sleeping. This is her DREAM. Appropriate music throughout. The Father exited and now returns: he is dressed in black,

hat and coat. He goes toward Rachel,
grabs her roughly around the neck
with his arm; he raises a knife in the
air.)

FATHER

How foolish, Rachel, to think our love for one another
should be greater than obedience to our Creator.

RACHEL

You're hurting me, Papa.

FATHER

(She squirms, he holds her firmly)

You've brought us to where we are, Rachel.

RACHEL
You're hurting me! Please let me go!

FATHER

No, my little Isaac. I'll do what is commanded of me.

RACHEL

God told you to sacrifice me, Papa?

FATHER

I must prepare you and wait.

(Puts down the knife, takes a long cord, one
end tied to his belt, and begins wrapping it
around her)

RACHEL

The binding is cutting into my skin.

(The voice of Rachel's Mother is heard)

VOICE

Abraham Gershon.

FATHER

Who calls? Here am I!

(Takes the knife and holds it up)

VOICE

Do not lay your hand upon your only child. Let your
daughter go.

FATHER

I have shown her the way. I have prepared her for the
sacrifice.

(He brings the knife down on Rachel.
She screams and then remains silent.
The Father disappears. A shrouded

figure, Rachel's Mother, gathers her up and carries her away. Lights down, then up on Hannah, Heidegger, and Jaspers)

Scene 12 Stage area

HANNAH

(To Heidegger)

You didn't take Rachel's critique seriously...

HEIDEGGER

Of course not. She's just a student, and not a very good one. She can never know the truth about me or philosophy.

(Extends his arms to collect Hannah and Jaspers)

Come. Stand with me.

(Hannah moves away with him; Jaspers does not; lights dim then up on Steven and Rachel)

Scene 13 Stage area

STEVEN

The committee rejected your paper?

RACHEL

Yes.

STEVEN

I'm sorry, Rachel. You must be very disappointed.

RACHEL

I'm disappointed and exhausted.

STEVEN

They'll ask you to make revisions.

RACHEL

I can make them. The more important revisions, in my life, have already been made.

STEVEN

Rachel?

RACHEL

What.

STEVEN

Do you think you could also...fall in love?

RACHEL

Again?

STEVEN

Yes. I'm back to plain.

RACHEL

How can I be sure you'll stay that way?

STEVEN

You'll be with me.

RACHEL

Is that a proposal?

STEVEN

Will you, Rachel? Will you marry me?

RACHEL

No!

STEVEN

Why?

RACHEL

You don't seem to understand how important PLAIN is!

STEVEN

I do! I really do! I just didn't understand how important it was for you.

RACHEL

Let me hear you say it.

STEVEN

Plain is important.

RACHEL

Tell me why.

STEVEN

Because truth matters.

RACHEL

It really does. At times, truth is more important than love. Now, what about all the people who don't understand the importance of plain? What about them?

STEVEN

Are you saying you want everyone to become plain?

RACHEL

That's for them to decide. But they deserve an opportunity.
We must begin as soon as possible.

STEVEN

Can't we begin by getting married?

(He takes her hand)

RACHEL

Yes.

(Her Father approaches)

Did you hear that, Papa? Steven and I are getting married!

FATHER

(Looks at Rachel with sadness)

I can't come to your wedding.

RACHEL

I know, Papa.

(Gives him a kiss on the cheek; Steven takes
his limp arm and shakes his hand)

Mama will be with me.

FATHER

I understand, Ruchele.

(Steven and the Father leave. Lights
dim to near darkness. Rachel goes to
her desk and picks up the telephone)

Scene 14 Rachel's room

RACHEL

Mama, it's me again.

(A dark figure emerges and stands facing her;
Rachel places the telephone on its base)

RACHEL'S MOTHER

What is it Rachel?

RACHEL

I can't close the big door in the sky all by myself.

RACHEL'S MOTHER

Of course you can't.

RACHEL

Do you think I did the right thing?

RACHEL'S MOTHER

Are you having doubts?

RACHEL

Not really.

RACHEL'S MOTHER

Being will no longer tempt us, Rachel.

RACHEL

Overcoming Heidegger and metaphysics is only half the problem.

RACHEL'S MOTHER

Disclosing the truth of Being was your warm-up exercise?

RACHEL

The door to the Supernatural is still open.

RACHEL'S MOTHER

Know what, Ruchele? The gods are tired of us. We work them mercilessly. Day and night, from every corner of our planet, demands are made which they cannot satisfy. They'd like to be free of us.

RACHEL

Freeing them would be the moral thing to do.

RACHEL'S MOTHER

Do it, Rachel!

(Pause)

Be patient with your father. Steven will make a good husband.

(Turns to leave, pauses)

And, Rachel, take a little time off to have children....

RACHEL

I hear you, Mama.

RACHEL'S MOTHER

That way we'll keep in touch.

(She disappears)

CURTAIN

www.ingramcontent.com/pod-product-compliance
Lightning Source LLC
Chambersburg PA
CBHW071717140626
46557CB00012B/911

9 780999 118795